ADVANCE PRAISE FOR *THE STREET BELONGS TO US*

"Pendleton Jiménez has painted an authentic picture of puberty with a light touch that is both respectful and endearing. Godoy's animated drawings, economical and evocative, add to the overall magic."
–LINDA SCHUYLER, co-creator and executive producer of the Degrassi franchise

"Full of humor and heart, *The Street Belongs to Us* is a beautiful and subversively queer story that probes the depths of intertwined human loss and connection."
–CORY SILVERBERG, author of *Sex Is a Funny Word*

"*The Street Belongs to Us* magically addresses gender, grief, pain, longing, and illness, all with a writing cadence that makes us love each character like family."
–JOIE LAMAR, author of *Mambo Lips*

"Beautifully written, this story of discovery and healing reminds us of the power of digging deep in both our own yards and in those of collective history."
–OLGA GARCÍA ECHEVERRÍA, author of *Falling Angels: Cuentos y Poemas*

"Look to *The Street Belongs to Us* for truth about kids, how they talk, how they mask and unmask their true feelings when faced with the hard truths of life. Truly affecting throughout to its deeply touching conclusion."
–CECILE PINEDA, author of *Entry without Inspection* and *Apology to a Whale*

"This delightful and sensitive story is both rich with emotion and with cultural and historical experiences. A book tenderly written, one to be cherished and enjoyed."
–GIANNA PATRIARCA, author of *Italian Women and Other Tragedies*

"*The Street Belongs to Us* creates a complex, rich, and beautiful world. Pendleton Jiménez shows us the beauty and importance of gender diversity and how kids can navigate the difficult and exciting changes that lie ahead."
–LISA SELIN DAVIS, author of *Tomboy: The Surprising History and Future of Girls Who Dare to Be Different*

"Such a joy to read! *The Street Belongs to Us* is a wholehearted, fun story that also focuses on navigating life's challenges like puberty and losing one's mom."
–CLAUDIA RODRIGUEZ, author of *Everybody's Bread*

"Super-duper wow! Pendleton Jiménez's *The Street Belongs to Us* is an ¡Oralé! amazing read. A joyful, captivating, corazón-tugging cuento. It is all queer fun, family love y cariño."
–VERÓNICA REYES, author of *Chopper! Chopper! Poetry from Bordered Lives*

THE STREET BELONGS TO US

KARLEEN PENDLETON JIMÉNEZ

ILLUSTRATED BY GABRIELA GODOY

ARSENAL PULP PRESS
VANCOUVER

ARSENAL PULP PRESS
Suite 202 – 211 East Georgia St.
Vancouver, BC V6A 1Z6
Canada
arsenalpulp.com

The publisher gratefully acknowledges the support of the Canada Council for the Arts and the
British Columbia Arts Council for its publishing program, and the Government of Canada,
and the Government of British Columbia (through the Book Publishing Tax Credit Program),
for its publishing activities.

Arsenal Pulp Press acknowledges the xʷməθkʷəy̓əm (Musqueam), Sḵwx̱wú7mesh (Squamish),
and səl̓ilwətaʔɬ (Tsleil-Waututh) Nations, custodians of the traditional, ancestral, and unceded
territories where our office is located. We pay respect to their histories, traditions, and
continuous living cultures and commit to accountability, respectful relations, and friendship.

This is a work of fiction. Any resemblance of characters to persons either living or deceased
is purely coincidental.

Cover illustrations by Gabriela Godoy
Cover and interior design by Jazmin Welch
Edited by Shirarose Wilensky
Copy edited by Linda Pruessen
Proofread by Alison Strobel

Printed and bound in Canada

Library and Archives Canada Cataloguing in Publication:
Title: The street belongs to us / Karleen Pendleton Jiménez ; illustrated by Gabriela Godoy.
Names: Pendleton Jiménez, Karleen, 1971– author. | Godoy, Gabriela, 1974– illustrator.
Identifiers: Canadiana (print) 20200329049 | Canadiana (ebook) 20200329065 |
  ISBN 9781551528403 (softcover) | ISBN 9781551528410 (HTML)
Classification: LCC PS8569.I425 S77 2021 | DDC jC813/.6—dc23

To my grandmother María Celia Tomasa Jiménez Giner Vda.
de Valles y Vda. de McCann, who filled me with her stories.

To my daughter Elena, who flings open the door each day
in search of adventure.

CONTENTS

OUR STREET

I live at 3618 Muscatel Avenue, where the wash makes the street bend. The wash is a big, deep cement stream that dribbles over algae. It is protected by a tall chain-link fence and a strip of desert filled with little prickly thorns. There are a few scrawny palm trees on our street, but mostly, the sky around us is empty. When the smog lifts you can see the radio towers all the way at the top of Mount Wilson.

On the other side of the wash, about a hundred yards away, is the freeway. There are so many cars on the freeway that you always hear a quiet hum, like the sound of the air-conditioning at the big pharmacy. There are so many cars on the freeway that the TV news guy says the exhaust is turning the rain into acid. He warns that it's eating away the steel that holds up the freeway itself. I think that's okay 'cause one day they'll cancel each other out. No more freeways and no more acid rain.

They say we shouldn't drink it, but Wolf and I tilt our heads back and open our mouths when the drops start falling. We run away if my mom sees us and starts hollering to stop. She wears a dress and heels, so she can't keep up with us. We sprint fast and breathe hard, and the smell of fresh mud pushes up into our noses. I'll be in trouble later, but it hardly ever rains in the San Gabriel Valley, so you don't want to miss your chance to taste a storm.

There are small fences between the front yards in our neighborhood, but nothing separates the yards from the street. Bushes, grass, and dirt bump into each other and make good hiding places. And the yards are perfect for Nerf football games. But you have to be careful because some drivers like to pretend that the bend on Muscatel Avenue is a racetrack. You have to stay out of the street. My cat, Vaquero, was killed by one of these race car drivers just two years ago.

But that was before I turned twelve, before Wolf and I waged our mud war, before the summer they tore up the street.

Alex Richardson-Salazar
Rosemead, Califas, Aztlán, 1984

chapter 1

DIGGING

"Nana, look! The trucks are here!" I shout.

"What trucks?" my nana answers, quickly setting down her coffee.

"For the sidewalks, remember? I'll get to skateboard all the way to school!"

"It's so loud, mija." She shakes her head. "It could be a trick. An invasion! Cuídate!"

"It's okay, Nana, I don't need to be careful," I say. "It's just concrete and gutters. And it'll be fun to watch them dig."

"Stop shouting and go outside, already!" My brother's voice, coming from his bedroom, is garbled. "I'm trying to sleep!"

Johnny is seventeen. He basically does three things. He sleeps, he complains, and he plays heavy metal really loud. I hope that doesn't happen to me when I become a teenager. It seems really boring.

I've been waiting for my front-row seat for the show. All the neighbors have been talking about it. The city has decided to rip up our whole street this summer. I throw off my pajamas and change into my striped shirt and jeans. Then I sit in the yard with a glass of milk and a piece of peanut butter toast gripped in my hands. It is the end of June, the time of year when the days trick you. It is cold in the morning and burning up in the afternoon. At nine a.m., the grass is cool and wet underneath me, but I barely notice. The trucks roll in yellow and red and silver. The machinery looks like muscles, big metal muscles.

"There're so many! Come quick!" I yell.

My nana leans over as she walks but still manages to drag an aluminum lawn chair out beside me. She is a tiny old lady with curled white hair, dark eyes, and a round, pretty face that used to get her hired to do commercials. She goes back inside the house and returns with her mug of coffee. Our neighbors from two doors over, Jaime and his brother, Mateo, are perched on their bicycles at the top of their driveway. Our other neighbors, from across the street—Diego, his mom, and his aunts—have pulled four chairs out

onto their porch. The women knit and talk and sometimes look up to see the digging.

I watch the metal claws push inside and crush the earth. Rocks and dirt crumble and fly.

"Wow, Nana! I wish my fists were that strong." I squeeze my hand into a ball and punch the grass.

My nana shakes her head. "Alex, I don't like that. La tierra nos cuida. It's dangerous to dig up the earth."

"If it's strong enough to take care of us, it's gotta be strong enough for me to dig it up," I answer back. "And then I could squish the mud into all kinds of shapes." I wave my hands in zigzag patterns.

"You think your shapes are better than the earth's?" My nana responds in her all-knowing way that means the answer is no.

"Nah, I don't mean that, Nana. I just want to be powerful enough to do it."

"Mija, even if you could, you might find things in the ground, things that were meant to be buried."

"Treasures?!" I get even more excited. "That would be cool."

"There are things that want to be found in the earth and things that don't." She sips her coffee. "I'm not worried about treasure. Things like gold and jewels want to be found. In fact, they're not so hard to find," she claims confidently. "Sometimes the ground above a treasure will glow, if you know how to look for it."

I want to ask if she's ever found a glowing treasure, but before I can get the words out, she says, "But sometimes old toys or dishes want to stay hidden and forgotten."

"Why?"

"Maybe they hold painful memories. Maybe a little girl once loved her dolly and her brothers threw it out in the garden so she couldn't find it. And then she cried and cried for over a year."

"Oh, Nana, that's awful. Did you know her?" She knows every story about every sad thing that ever happened from California to México.

"I knew her brother, and he was a real creep. He used to pull the girls' trenzas at school." She shakes her head disapprovingly.

I know what she's talking about. "That's how it all started with Diego. He grabbed Maria's hair, but the teacher didn't see it. That's why I elbowed him, and–"

But my nana is in her own world and not really listening to my story about Diego. She isn't done with her stories. "Or maybe the dishes were a wedding gift to a young couple, but the husband disappeared the week after the ceremony," she continues. "Nobody was ever sure whether he ran off to join the war or had some kind of accident while walking between the villages. He could have been attacked by bandits." Her eyes get big at "bandits."

"Whoa!" I exclaim. I know she's making the story good and scary for me.

She shakes her head. "The broken dishes buried deep in the ground would be reminders of the mystery of the man and the pain of the woman."

"I remember that one. Wasn't that your tía Catalina?" My nana always repeats her stories, and I already know many of them by heart.

"She never remarried," she says, and sighs.

"She died too young of a broken heart," I say, because I know it's the next, and last, line of her story. I've heard it

so many times, but I don't really know how you can die just because your heart hurts. I don't think that part is actually true.

My nana is sick with Alzheimer's, which makes her forget things. She doesn't seem sick, though. She looks at the TV or the living room or the street and daydreams a lot. Her daydreaming mostly doesn't hurt anyone, but if she were a kid at my school, it would really irritate the teachers. At home you can daydream as long as you want without getting into trouble.

Crash! The big claws strike our yard a foot away from the rosebushes. I jump into the air with my fists out, ready to fight.

"My father planted those flowers!" I scream.

The machine is too loud for the driver to hear me, though, and after it dumps a load of dirt, it comes back to plunge into our grass again. My nana takes her slipper off and climbs up from her chair. She holds the slipper in the air, waves it around, and heads toward the machine.

I gasp. "No, Nana, no!"

She's going to get hurt. I try to grab her dress to stop her, but she keeps moving forward. She's very strong, even though she's so short and old.

"You think you can take our land with your big, loud machine?!" she shouts. "You're not taking anything from me! I survived the Mexican Revolution! A cannonball went right through my roof when I was only three years old!"

"Nana, stop!" I scream.

The guy with the hard hat in the little window of the machine doesn't see us. He makes it whirl around again–but only to stretch out the metal claws once more. I'm sure he's going to knock right into my nana's shins. I cover my eyes.

Suddenly, the noise stops.

I open my eyes. The construction man's eyes are open too wide, and he is gripping the steering wheel tight.

My nana is standing right next to his machine's huge metal tracks, hitting its window with her slipper.

chapter 2

WOLF

"Nana! Be careful!" I run up and reach for her elbow, trying to pull her back.

The loud noise of the digging machine has turned to silence, but my nana's hands are still clenched into fists.

"Qué barbaridad!" she shouts. "Those are her father's roses! He pruned them every Sunday."

The construction man wipes his sweaty face. "I'm sorry, señora," he says about five times.

She shakes her finger at him. "You better not touch our flowers."

The driver assures her that the machines won't go near the rosebushes.

My nana whispers angry words under her breath while leading me back to the house. That's when I decide I have to act.

I run in the front door and yank the receiver from the green wall phone. It's not actually green anymore, but I still think of it that way. It's covered in thick white brushstrokes. A couple of years ago my mom announced that we had to move into the eighties, and so far that has meant getting rid of all the avocado-colored decor. She painted the door, the wall, and the phone, only I don't think you're supposed to paint telephones. Now I can only use it when the phone number doesn't include a six, because the white paint made that button stick. And my mom doesn't like it so much when we use the phone in her bedroom. Luckily, Wolf's number doesn't have a six, and I have it memorized, so I can call him quickly in emergency cases like today.

"Hi ... is Wolf there?" I speak awkwardly because a woman answers the phone. I'm not used to there being a woman at Wolf's house.

Then I hear a long drawn out "Heeeeyyyy." Wolf always answers all cool, like he was expecting my call.

"It's Alex. You need to come over. The machines have arrived and they're awesome. They look like giant metal bugs! Anyway, who was that woman who answered the phone?"

Even though Wolf McCann is my best friend, I still get nervous talking to him on the phone. I hurry to get all my words out and forget to breathe.

"I'm coming." He hangs up without answering my question.

Wolf doesn't talk much on the phone. It's almost like he doesn't know what to say after his first hey. I don't mind, though, because I know he'll be here, on my lawn and then in my house, on our broken street, in ten minutes flat. His house is next to the freeway, too, only three blocks over to the west.

I run to my room and explain to Hops the Kangaroo that Wolf is coming to help me figure out what to do about the street being torn up. My dad gave Hops to me before he left us. He works for Amtrak, and one day he was extra nice to an Australian tourist. The tourist asked my dad if he had any kids, and when he found out about me and Johnny, the tourist gave Hops to my dad as a gift for one of us. Johnny was already too old for a stuffed animal, so that's how I got to have him.

I head to the bathroom and brush the peanut butter out of my teeth. Looking in the mirror, I see my short brown hair sticking straight up on top. It's my fault. I tried cutting it myself because my nana won't cut it short enough for me. I pointed to an actor on TV whose hair was shaved on the sides and back, exactly how I wanted mine. My nana nodded and said she'd do it, but then she didn't shave it at all. She said this was the girl version of the same haircut, like it was an official thing. I don't buy it. She just doesn't think girls should have short hair. So I found her clippers that night after everyone went to bed and cleared the hair away. My mom got really annoyed and said it was patchy. The only reason I'm not in real trouble is because it's summertime, so there's no school and nobody around to really care.

The doorbell rings, and Johnny lets out another groan from his bedroom. "The whole point of summer is not having to wake up!" he yells.

I run past his room and open the door before my nana can get up from her chair in the living room. Wolf stands before me in his uniform.

Every single day, Wolf wears a white T-shirt and camouflage pants. Around his neck, he wears a thin gold chain with a tiny gold cross. His mom gave him that cross before she died, and he never takes it off. He wears black army boots and a green military cap over his curly brown hair. His hair is very thick and feels like a brush if you touch it. His green eyes look even greener underneath the cap.

Wolf used to wear all kinds of different clothes, but since his mom died, he only wears his uniform. Kids at school make fun of him for wearing the same thing every day, calling him Rambo Boy. He doesn't mind so much because he says he is just like Rambo from the movie: able to survive on his own, even if everyone in the world turns against him. In a very serious voice, he tells them he is a soldier, and he is wearing his uniform. They usually stop making fun of him then.

It really bugs the teachers and the principal that Wolf wears the same thing every day and calls himself a soldier. They have meetings to try to get him to change his clothes. He refuses and they get madder, and the principal even suspended him once over it. I don't ever bug Wolf about his uniform. It's what he wants, so I don't get what the big deal is.

It's like with my clothes. I like to wear my brother's hand-me-down wide-striped shirts and blue jeans. And I have a favorite pair of gray jeans for when I want to look dressed up. It's how I feel good, but some kid or grown-up is always asking me why I don't wear girls' clothes. Not Wolf, though. He leaves me alone, and I leave him alone.

We go outside to see the machines. Wolf sits on the lawn next to me, watching the steel limbs slice through the street. His eyes are big and intensely focused like when he watches TV. I know he won't hear me if I talk, but I can't help it.

"So, who was that woman who answered the phone?" I ask him.

No response.

"Is one of your aunts visiting?"

No response.

His chin is resting on his knees as he watches one of the machines burrow into the land right in front of my yard. He's not going to answer, so I might as well drop it and think about something else.

I look back at the machines. As they turn the pavement into crumbled-up bits of dirt, I suddenly feel incredibly happy.

"Wolf, the cars won't be able to zoom around here all summer," I say.

"Mhmm," he utters, not listening.

"And grown-ups won't want to hang out in the dirt."

"Yep," he answers, still not listening.

"Do you understand the ramifications of this?" Big words seem to have a way of getting his attention, so I throw them in when it's important.

"What?"

"Wolf, it could be an all-kid street."

"Wait, that's true."

Now I've got him. He's nodding slowly, imagining our future. "Then there's no time to waste." He stands up, scratching his chin, and begins pacing back and forth on the lawn. "We need to plan this out, grab strongholds quick, lay out paths."

"What?"

Now it's me who doesn't clue in. But this happens a lot. I don't really know military language. I am not a committed soldier like Wolf, or Rambo. I'm more of an accidental soldier like Hawkeye Pierce, a doctor who got drafted into the Korean War on the TV show *M*A*S*H*. He's very smart and funny but not so good at being a soldier and gets into trouble. I think maybe something like that happened to my dad. Maybe he got shipped off by the government to go fight in a war, even though he didn't want to. He's been gone three years and I don't know when he's coming back. I don't think my mom knows either, but she won't really talk about it.

I got drafted by Wolf because he's my best friend and he only wants to play soldiers since his mom died. But I don't have to go anywhere far away or get hurt or anything. Wolf just wears his army uniform and gives commands, and then we have pretend battles with other kids, think up compli- cated strategies, and look for new places to hang out. Our version of being soldiers isn't such hard work.

"Look, Alex, this is serious," Wolf says. "The other kids will move in quick. If we don't stake out our territory, Diego and Jaime and who knows who else will take over."

He looks out across the piles of dirt and walks over to the large hole the machines dug right in front of my yard. It's a trench approximately six feet deep by six feet long by three feet wide.

Wolf points down and shouts to me, "This is it!"

"What is it?" I ask, alarmed.

"Our headquarters." He nods confidently. "Get a ladder."

I take a ladder from the garage out to our trench. It fits perfectly into the left side and Wolf climbs down. I follow after him quickly. Inside the trench it is very quiet and smells like mud. It's wet and cool, like we've traveled to a different country. Somewhere magical. Like a cave behind a waterfall.

Suddenly, it feels like there won't be enough air, and I start breathing faster. I hold my hands up to my throat. I gasp, "I can't breathe!"

Wolf pushes me on the back.

"Hey, what was that for?" I shout and hit him back on the shoulder.

"So you'd stop breathing weird," he says. "There's no time for one of your panic attacks. We've got work to do."

I stand still and cross my arms.

Wolf stares at me. "Hey man, sorry, okay?" he says. He looks me straight in the eye and breathes in a big, deep breath, puffing out his chest. "See, there's plenty of air."

I give him a dirty look. It is very irritating when he pushes me, but it does seem to stop my freak-outs. It's never clear to me, though, whether he's trying to help me, or if he just wants me to do something for him. At least he notices when I start breathing funny. He's the only one who can tell.

"We need supplies," Wolf says.

I consider this. "We could raid the camping gear in the garage," I offer. "But we can't make too much noise, or my nana or Johnny could catch us and tell my mom."

Wolf nods and we climb up the ladder and run quickly and quietly like cats over to the garage. I open the door slowly and switch on the light. There are five women in swimsuits on posters beaming back at me from the far wall. This is what Johnny calls art.

"Yuck!" I say and switch off the light, fast.

"What did you see?" Wolf asks.

"Um ... ah, it was an old, squished, moldy banana," I say. "Trust me, you don't want to look at it. It's over near the wall."

The light coming in from the door is enough to let us see what we need. We grab two folding chairs, two sleeping bags, a flashlight, a camping canteen, and some ropes and clips to hold our stuff out of the mud when it rains. I sneak into the house and grab the fancy silver binoculars my dad gave me, as well as my journal so that I can take battle notes when I don't have anything else to do. On *M*A*S*H*, there are plenty of episodes where the soldiers get bored, Hawk-eye especially.

We make four trips back and forth without a sound. On our fifth, I spot two sheets of tin that could cover the top of one side of our trench. I carry one of them out on top of my head, but it starts to wobble and I drop it with a crash onto the driveway.

I give Wolf a terrified look, and then we run and climb down into our trench to wait.

"Oh no!" I gasp and point at my nana, who is walking out of the house and toward our hole.

We crouch down in the bottom of the trench, and I squeeze my eyes shut tight. I hear her footsteps walk right up to the edge. Maybe she won't notice ...

"Alex?" she asks.

"Nope," I answer.

"But I think that's you, Alex," she responds.

"Not at all," I confirm.

"And that's your little friend Lobito."

Wolf groans.

"She's trying to trick you," I whisper. "Don't fall for it."

But Wolf can't help himself. "Doña Salazar, I told you that my name is Wolf. Or Lobo, if you want. I like how that sounds, too." He sighs. "But not Lobito. I'm not small, and I'm not cute."

"Mira," my nana chuckles, "see now. It is the two of you."
She scrunches her eyebrows. "I'm not so sure about you
hiding down there."

"But Nana," I say, "I haven't found anything bad buried
down here. Just some rocks."

She bends down and pats one of the walls. "Hmm, it
does feel pretty solid, honey," she says approvingly. "When
I was a girl in the war, we had to hide in the caves."

I peek up at her for this story and add, "After the cannonball went through your house."

"Yes, mija." She nods and ducks, holding her hands over her head to protect herself. "It shot splinters all over us."

"Whoa!" Wolf exclaims. "Was it exciting?"

"It was mostly scary, Lobito," she says and lowers her arms.

Wolf is about to correct her about his name again, when my nana raises her finger and walks quickly back into the house.

"Oh no." Wolf chews his lip. "Do you think she's gonna tell on us?"

"I hope not," I say. "Maybe she just remembered her telenovela is on."

Wolf climbs back out of our trench and uses the sheet of tin to cover half of it. He explains how it'll make a strong shelter but still give us plenty of room to look out for potential enemies.

We don't have any real enemies that I know of, but I don't say this because Wolf is so excited about our new trench. The closest thing we have to enemies are Diego from across the street and Jamie from two doors down. Four years ago they broke into my house through the cat door and ate a whole box of Ding Dongs. I was really mad because my dad bought them for us (my mom would never let us have junk food like that), and now he's gone, and the Ding Dongs are gone, and we probably won't ever get any more. Their parents yelled at them and made them apologize and pay my parents back for the Ding Dongs, so the whole thing was supposed to be fixed. But we never did get any new Ding Dongs, and in my mind that makes them archenemies. Still, we're only talking about two dollars in damages. So they're the ones we usually battle, but the truth is we mostly fight for fun and nobody actually gets hurt.

We take some time to set up all of our equipment and stake out our spots. I lie on one of the sleeping bags spread underneath the tin part of the trench. I wedge the handle of a flashlight into the trench wall, click it on, and open up my journal to take notes. Wolf borrows my binoculars and perches on the second rung of the ladder, his eyes just an inch above ground level, ready to report any suspicious behavior.

After a few minutes of nothing happening, Wolf announces, "We've got to make some mud balls."

"What for?" I ask, bothered by the idea of moving off my cozy sleeping bag.

"A defensive artillery stockpile," he proclaims.

"What does that mean?" I wonder aloud.

"We have to be prepared for any and all attacks," Wolf answers with great seriousness.

I nudge Wolf to one side of the ladder and climb up next to him. I raise my head out of the hole and scan the street. The five-year-old Mahoney twins are down the street riding around on their big wheel tricycles, but other than that, there's nobody in sight.

"No one's even around," I say.

"Not yet," he answers.

I shake my head doubtfully but climb out of the trench and grab the garden hose. Wolf follows, and we get to work digging and rolling the mud beside our trench.

My nana walks out of the house again, this time with a bag in her arms. When she reaches us, she gazes at the metal sheets over our trench. "Your little home is so beautiful," she says. "Like the houses with tin roofs near the border, right before you walk over into El Paso."

Wolf gets serious again. "It's not beautiful, Doña Salazar," he informs her. "It's a very strong defensive shield."

My nana doesn't really pay attention to him, though. "When I was a kid, there were so many tin roofs that sparkled together in the desert sun that I thought it was the ocean."

"That must've been so pretty, Nana," I say, because I love the ocean.

Wolf gives me a dirty look. I shrug. Even though my nana was a little kid when she came to America, a lot of the things she can still remember happened in México.

"It wasn't the ocean, but the sparkling was the first thing I remember seeing as we escaped the war and walked right into the valley of Aztlán," she declares. "Pay attention when the ground sparkles."

"Where's Aztlán?" Wolf asks.

"She means when she crossed the border into America," I explain.

"Only the Mexican part of the United States, mija." She smiles.

"What do you mean the Mexican part of America? The Mexican-American War claimed the new territories for the United States in 1848," Wolf asserts. He reads information books all the time. Social studies and science are his only good grades at school. I try to avoid books, especially during summertime.

My nana pats Wolf on the head. "They've never really taken the land away from us, though."

"But when President Polk invaded México–" Wolf starts.

"You'll need provisions," my nana says, interrupting him, because she is all done listening to his facts. She lowers the bag into my arms. It's full of candy bars, chips, and two little burritos she must've just made for us. "We didn't have enough food in the caves," she explains. "That was miserable."

"Wow! Thanks, Nana," I say.

"Whoa, yeah, that's really nice of you, Doña Salazar," says Wolf, who has suddenly lost his defensiveness and is grabbing a chocolate bar.

"But always remember to bring the snack bag into the house at the end of the day," she warns us. "Remember when that big rat ate up your whole chocolate bar in the backyard, Alex?"

I nod sheepishly. "Yes, Nana."

"We will follow your orders, ma'am," Wolf says and salutes her.

The salute makes my nana grin, and she heads back to the house.

Wolf sighs. "Do you think your mom will be that nice about our headquarters?"

I shrug and rinse the mud from our hands with the hose. I sit down next to our new stockpile of mud balls, unwrap the foil on one of the burritos, and take a bite. Wolf sits next to me and opens the other one. The eggs and potatoes and cheese and salsa are warm and perfect. I feel lucky that my nana is here to help take care of me. My mom has to work way too much to make me a snack like this in the middle of the afternoon.

I look over at our trench. "My mom would be mad if she saw what we took from the garage, but I'm betting she's not going to think to look inside."

Wolf nods.

My mom's too busy these days with work and school and community associations and books and phone calls. She doesn't have enough time or energy to look inside holes.

chapter 3

SIDEWALKS

I don't recognize our street anymore. It's turned into a big mess of piles of brown dirt and deep holes. It's not like the ground in the desert, where the rocks and plants seem settled into their right spots. It's more like a garden right before you plant the seeds. Everything torn up and ready for new life to grow.

The street fills up with all the neighborhood kids during the day. We flood the ground with our garden hoses and ride our bikes through the mud in an enormous figure eight. We follow the path so tightly that it makes a permanent groove in our street.

It has been a week since the day of the digging machines, and they haven't come back. Some grown-ups are complaining, but not my mom. She is mostly away at work and doesn't really spend much time on the street.

"They're giving us sidewalks. It'll help the moms pushing strollers and the people with wheelchairs," she explains to Johnny and me at dinner.

The city promises that everything will be fixed before the fall, but it doesn't look like it.

"They probably ran out of money," Mrs Vega from next door yelled over our fence last night when my mom was outside watering the bushes. "This city doesn't know how to take care of money."

Mrs Vega has gotten her station wagon stuck in the mud twice while trying to get into her driveway. I don't see what the big deal is, though. She just honks and all the kids come out from wherever they are on the street, and we push and push her wagon until she pulls free. Then we cheer and go back to playing. I don't care if they ever put sidewalks in.

"With sidewalks, you'll be able to ride your bikes safely, away from the cars," Mom tells us while we're eating our chicken.

I don't know why she bothers telling Johnny this. He's five years older than me and doesn't do anything safely. Sidewalks won't change that. Johnny's long dark hair covers half his face so that it's hard to see his eyes. Mostly what

I see is Johnny's mouth, and he doesn't even stop to nod between bites of his dinner.

I leap up and grab my skateboard, which is leaning against the wall. I jump on, bend my knees, and hold my arms out like I'm surfing in the ocean. "Look, Mom, I'll be able to skateboard all the way to school."

My nana claps. My mom smiles but then remembers her rule. "No riding in the house, Alex." She says it softly, though, so I know I'm not really in trouble.

I hop off my skateboard and return to my seat. I am about to take a bite when I notice something awful. "Hey, my chicken leg is gone!"

Johnny starts giggling. He's chewed half the meat off it already. "Here, you want it back?" he taunts and tosses it onto my plate.

"Ewww, gross," I say and throw it back at him.

He ducks, and it misses him and slides across the linoleum floor. He laughs harder.

"Stop fighting at the table! And don't throw food!" my mom shouts. Now I know she is actually angry.

"He started it," I say, defending myself.

"He started it." Johnny mimics me in a high, whiny voice.

"Stop it, Johnny," Mom says curtly.

I give him a smug little smile.

Johnny stops laughing and looks down at his plate. He gobbles the last three bites of his dinner and gets up to leave. He looks at my mom, says, "Dinners were better with Dad," and walks toward his bedroom.

My mom's eyes get shiny. I look at her, but I don't know what to do.

My nana suddenly picks up where we left off, like nothing happened. "With sidewalks you can roller-skate. Roller-skating was my favorite thing when I was a little girl," she tells me. "I would skate all the way from the Mission down to the big public library at the Civic Center in San Francisco. I remember when–"

"Weren't the steep hills dangerous?" my mom says before my nana can launch into a story that would take up the rest of dinner for sure. I figure my mom has three reasons for interrupting: 1) She doesn't like my nana repeating her stories all the time; 2) She believes most things are dangerous and doesn't want my nana encouraging me to do those dangerous things; and 3) She's still mad at Johnny, but he's not at the table to fight with anymore. My nana is still here and always ready to argue with my mom.

"Nope, I was very skilled. And besides, it was good exercise," my nana explains, and smiles with all her teeth showing. My nana brings up exercise whenever she wants to irritate my mom.

My mom rolls her eyes. "Good exercise won't help if you're in the hospital with a broken leg."

My nana wipes her lips politely with her napkin and says sweetly, "You'll end up in the hospital anyway if you get too fat from no exercise."

"I'm fine, Mother," my mom says curtly.

"But men might be more interested in you if you lost some weight," my nana pushes.

"Plenty of men like me well enough," my mom answers sternly. "And I don't actually need one to support me."

My nana tells my mom she is too fat at least once a week. I love my nana a ton, but I wish she wouldn't say that. Who cares if my mom is fat? Who cares if anyone is fat? I don't. I used to live inside her big stomach. My nana hurts my mom's feelings, and sometimes they get into fights about it. My mom looks like a photocopy of my nana, only bigger and with dark brown hair instead of white. I think my nana looks at my mom and sees a fat version of herself, and it makes her say those mean comments to my mom. I tell my nana and my mom they are both really pretty, but it doesn't stop them from fighting.

Tonight, my mom shakes her head, wipes her mouth, and stands up. "Just be careful when the sidewalks come, mija."

When my mom gets home from work, she is very tired. She's in charge of all the money at the schools to make sure the teachers and the principals and the secretaries get paid, and the buildings get fixed, and they don't go bankrupt. She doesn't feel like arguing with my nana. She rinses her plate and puts it in the dishwasher. Then she leaves the kitchen in her big flowered skirt, with a book under her arm, and goes to her bedroom.

I wish my mom didn't have to work so much, but I'm kind of glad she hasn't noticed our trench. She would think the trench was dangerous, too. Maybe the walls would cave in. Maybe somebody wouldn't see the trench and would fall on top of our heads. But nothing bad has happened so far.

Wolf says we have to stay camped out in our trench. With all the dirt and kids around all day long, he predicts a great battle is coming soon. Actually, he's hoping for a battle. Being a kid living in the suburbs hasn't really given him too many opportunities to be a soldier.

chapter 4

YOU'RE GONNA PAY FOR THIS

Wolf and I peer out of the trench and watch as Diego's older brother, Tony, skids in circles on the muddy street in his black vw Bug. He installed roll bars inside so that if he does ever flip over, the roof won't cave in. He speeds up, slams on the brakes, and skids into the turn. The car makes loud screeching sounds and shoots mud in every direction. The Villagrana brothers a few doors up run inside their house to get away. Tony knocks goop all over my dad's roses, and Diego goes into hysterics, giggling and pointing from across the street.

"Teenagers are the worst." I shake my head.

"Something is wrong with their brains," Wolf explains. "It's science."

"I hope I don't get dumb like that," I fret.

"Me too," Wolf says. "I hope he stops soon."

Tony shows no signs of stopping. He spins out and nearly crashes over the edge of the wash. He runs over a bush and dents the fence. He gets out of the car, checks the damage, and laughs.

"I don't think it's such a good idea that they let teenagers drive cars," I mutter.

Our perfectly beautiful dirt street has been taken over by a single idiot. The grown-ups are still at work, so there's nobody around to tell him to stop.

Unless? Hmm.

"Wolf?"

"Yeah?" he says, cringing as Tony pulls pieces of a thorny bush out from the wheel well above his tire. Tony yelps and kicks the bush when the prickles puncture his hand.

"We could try to get Johnny to stop him," I suggest.

He shakes his head. "Then we'll have two teenagers to deal with."

"Maybe they'd cancel each other out?"

Tony hops back into his car and starts the engine, giving it a good revving.

Wolf nods. "Go."

I can vaguely hear the deep thrumming of Johnny's bass guitar coming from the garage. Last year, Johnny cleaned

up the garage and made it into his band's practice space, covering the walls with blankets so that the music wouldn't be too loud for the neighbors. I think it's the only thing he's ever cleaned. He calls it his sound studio. When he's in there, no one is allowed to interrupt him. But this is a special case.

I knock. "Johnny?"

Thum, thum thum thum, thumming Metallica bass solos, endlessly.

"Johnny?" I call again and open the door. "It's important."

"What?!" he yells.

"Tony's driving his car around like crazy," I blurt out. "I'm afraid he's going to hit something."

Johnny shrugs. "That's got nothing to do with me," he says and slams the door in my face.

"Argh!" I shout, but he's gone back to his guitar now.

I wish Johnny wasn't so mad all the time. He wasn't like that before he started high school. He would boss me around and flip me over and stuff, but he wasn't in a bad mood most days. He hasn't really hung out with me since our dad left.

He says it's my mom's fault that my dad left, but I feel like he blames me, too. My mom and dad used to get into a lot of fights over me. Like when I stopped eating peas because they made me feel like barfing and my dad told me I couldn't leave the table until I ate the pile on my plate. My mom said I didn't have to eat them and they started arguing. I ran to my room and Johnny yelled after me to "stop being such a baby." My parents kept right on fighting. Maybe it was my fault that he left.

I walk slowly back over to the trench and lower myself in next to Wolf. Tony drives around the corner and out of sight. I think we have a reprieve, until I hear his engine revving, over and over. I hear the thum thum thum of Johnny's guitar together with the rev rev rev of Tony's engine, and I'm still thinking about those dumb peas, and I feel sick to my stomach.

Tony slides into gear and screeches back around the corner and onto our street. He's going way too fast. When he finally pounds the brakes, the car doesn't stop. It does a sideways glide across the mud, up a curve, through the Vega's bushes, and bang! Into the corner of our garage.

"Whoa!" yells Wolf.

"No way!" screams Diego.

The three of us run to the side of the garage to see a new two-foot hole and crumbling plaster.

Tony gets out to take a look and says, "Oh crap, man." He doesn't appear to be hurt, but he's shaking his head and cursing as he stares at the damage to the hood of his vw.

Johnny comes out of the garage to find the group of us staring at the wreckage.

"Dude!" Johnny exclaims, his voice full of anger and disbelief. "That's my sound studio."

"Uh, sorry," Tony answers lamely.

Diego pipes up, protecting his brother. "I saw it all and it wasn't his fault."

"Oh yeah, it was!" Wolf retorts.

I nod. "It totally was."

"You better fix it," Johnny warns Tony.

"It's like he said, it wasn't my fault." Tony looks squarely at Johnny. "It's all the loose dirt in the road. The city's to blame."

"You mean this dirt?" Johnny says. He picks up a chunk of smashed bits of lawn, grass, and dirt hanging together and flings it in Tony's face.

"Hey!" Tony screams. "I'll get you for that." He grabs some mud, while Diego crouches down and digs into the ground.

Johnny turns on his heel and quickly heads into the house before they can hit him back. Wolf and I run and leap into our trench. We gather up six of the mud balls we had stored and get ready for action. Johnny comes out of the house wearing an army helmet and turns on the garden hose.

Tony shouts from the other side of the garage, "Where are you, girly-girl metalhead with the long pretty hair?!"

But when Tony and Diego come around the garage looking for Johnny, chunks of dirt clutched in their fingers, Wolf and I pelt them with our mud balls while Johnny sprays them down with the hose. Diego and Tony cringe and yelp, trying to brush the mess off their clothes. They look at us in our trench, and Johnny with the hose, and retreat.

"We're gonna get you back, bad," Diego threatens as he runs across the street.

Tony gets in his smooshed car, lurches in reverse out of the hole he punched in the garage, and parks in his own driveway.

"You can't just crash into people's houses," I yell at him.

"Yeah," Wolf says, "that's trespassing!"

Wolf and I shake our heads, disgusted.

Johnny comes over to examine our whole trench setup, looking from us to our chairs to our snacks to our mud balls.

"Awesome," he announces. He takes his army helmet off and places it over my narrow head. "Do some damage."

"Thanks, Johnny," I say, surprised. Our cousin Chucky gave him the helmet after Vietnam, and Johnny doesn't usually let it out of his sight. I never know when my brother is going to be nice, or why.

Johnny turns to go, and then stops. "Wait."

"Yeah?" Wolf says.

"Give me one of those chocolate bars," he demands.

I hand him one and he heads back to the garage. His guitar thrumming starts again, louder now through the hole in the wall.

My nana emerges from the house, looking bewildered, and comes over to our trench. "I hear music in the sky, mija," she says.

"It's just Johnny playing his guitar," I explain, pointing. "But there's a new hole in the garage that's letting the sound out."

My nana walks around to the side of the garage and gasps when she sees the damage. She crouches down and creeps quickly back to us.

"Was it Pancho Villa's army or the Federales who fired the cannonball?" she asks in a panic.

"No, Nana," I explain. "It was just Tony and his stupid car."

"Is he a general?" she asks.

"No, he's a teenager," I say.

"And a bad driver," Wolf adds.

"There's no war?" My nana wants to confirm.

"Nope." Wolf sighs sadly.

"Are you sure?" she asks suspiciously and peers up and down the street.

"Nana," I say, "the Mexican Revolution is over. It was, like, seventy years ago. Pancho Villa and the federal soldiers are all dead now. They can't bomb you anymore."

"Oh, okay," my nana says and scratches her head. "Who won?"

I shrug. "I don't know if anyone did."

"Venustiano Carranza," Wolf contributes. "And then he became the president."

"Hmm." My nana nods. "I didn't see that coming."

My nana turns away and begins to gently bob her head to the guitar strokes. "The music's nice," she says.

She walks back to the house and returns with a folding chair and a sun umbrella. She sets herself up next to the garage, tapping her foot to Johnny's strumming.

Wolf and I spend the rest of the afternoon manufacturing mud ball grenades and drawing up battle strategies that we store at the far end of our headquarters. It is very peaceful for a couple of hours, until my mom comes home.

The second she turns off the engine, she shouts, "What the heck happened to the garage?!"

My nana tries to calm her, reassuring her it wasn't a cannonball.

"Johnny!" she yells. "What have you done to the garage?"

Johnny comes out and yells, "Stop blaming me for every-thing!" He storms off into the house.

Wolf and I sneak out of our trench.

"Mom?" I say quietly behind her. I scare her accidentally, and she jumps a little.

"Oh, Alex, it's just you," she says. "Where did you two come from?"

Instead of answering that question I defend my brother. "It wasn't Johnny," I say. "Tony crashed into the garage with his car." I point over to his dented-up vw Bug in his family's driveway.

"It was totally Tony's fault," Wolf adds.

"Unbelievable!" my mom complains loudly. "I can't even go to work without coming home to a hole in the garage."

All of a sudden it seems like a bigger deal than it had a couple of hours ago.

"This is going to cost a fortune to fix! Did nobody think to call me?" she asks, exasperated.

When the crash happened, I thought we were pretty brave and successful defenders, throwing mud balls at Tony and Diego in revenge. Now I look down at the driveway and feel guilty.

My mom heads into the house to call the police. Wolf ducks out before they arrive and remember who he is. He is already on their radar after throwing a notebook at the principal last year. It smacked him right on the nose, and then everyone freaked out because of the blood. Wolf promises to come back tomorrow morning, though.

A helicopter circles the street twice before flying away.

My mom looks up. "The police send the helicopters for everything in Rosemead." She shakes her head. "The damage is already done!"

My mom and I stand beside our garage while she points at the crumbled stucco, complaining to the police who have arrived in their patrol car. When the officers head across the street to get the other side of the story, we glare over at the family on their front lawn. Tony pretends to limp, probably to get the officers to feel sorry for him.

"He wasn't hurt!" I exclaim, outraged.

We stay and keep watch to see if they have any other tricks up their sleeves, but it's mostly a boring police officer writing a bunch of words in his notebook. We can't hear anything this far away.

As soon as the police head off and we're finally about to go back inside our house, Diego calls me over. We step away from the grown-ups so that they won't overhear us.

"What do you want?" I whisper.

"You're gonna pay for this," he answers. "The police are blaming Tony."

"Pay for what?" I say. "It was his fault."

"Police don't know anything," he responds. "And besides, we still need to get you back for those mud balls you threw this afternoon."

"You're on," I answer.

"Tomorrow, first thing," he declares. "The battle begins."

chapter 5

BATTLE

07:55. I call Wolf and alert him to Diego's battle cry. He was still sleeping when I called and mutters, "They drew first blood, not me."

I frown. "Are you dreaming that you're Rambo again?"

He mumbles, "I won't surrender."

"Wolf." I raise my voice. "Wake up! Get ahold of yourself."

"Wha? What's going on?" Wolf says, finally sounding awake.

"Diego is planning to battle us this morning, and I need you over here ASAP," I plead.

08:25. My mom carries her coffee mug out to the car and leaves for work.

08:59. Wolf arrives at my place in uniform. My nana cooks up our papas con huevos burrito rations and wraps them in foil for us. We head out to the trench.

09:33. The rations are already gone. Wolf perches near the top of the ladder. He is wearing Johnny's army helmet and staring intently through my silver binoculars. (It's very irritating that he takes such long turns with them.)

Finally, Wolf speaks. "Diego's dad is approaching his vehicle. Now he's entering it."

I am writing this down, recording important enemy movements in my field journal.

"He started his motor and is backing out of the driveway," Wolf states quickly.

"Yes, sir." I wait for further information. I wait longer. I get bored. "Captain McCann, you're supposed to tell me when he's driven away, too."

We can't have a battle until Diego's dad has left for work. He probably wouldn't like our game. He is the maintenance man at the school, and he gets angry at kids for breaking things and making messes. Actually, he doesn't like kids playing any games that are too loud, and it turns out every game we ever play is too loud. My mom says he fought in Vietnam and it hurt his head, so we should stay away from him.

"I'm well aware of that, Sergeant Salazar," Wolf says. "It's just, he forgot something and went back inside the house."

"Ugh. What's with him? He forgets something every single day." It's so frustrating. Didn't his mother yell at him not to forget things like my mom does? Wouldn't he know better now that he's a grown-up? Some mornings *I* want to yell at him because I know he's forgotten something, but I don't dare. "Well, what is it today?"

"His lunch box."

Wolf waits and watches for a few moments, and then makes a quick hand signal with his fist to announce that Diego's dad is finally gone. Wolf said we needed to have hand signs, even though we can hear each other in the trench. He says you never know when you might need to communicate without making a sound. What you do is squeeze your fist fast, and then drop it down like you're pounding an invisible bug.

09:42. Diego runs out of his house, carrying a big plastic bag. He carefully slides into a little trench in front of his house. Jaime, who lives around the curve of our street, suddenly appears, running toward Diego's trench. He jumps inside with Diego. They may be conspiring against us, but their trench is not as big as ours and maybe only half as deep. This is excellent because it means we are twice as likely to hit them with our mud balls.

10:15. "I am Fernando Valenzuela, with the strongest pitching arm in Major League Baseball," Diego shouts while Jaime cheers.

"What are you talking about?" I lift my head up out of the trench and yell.

That's when the crashing begins. We discover the contents of Diego's plastic bag when a soft, heavy, round, pink balloon ruptures upon contact with the top of my head. Water splashes all the way down my face. This initial projectile is followed in short order by a wet blue bomb ricocheting off our tin roof and bursting all over Wolf. And then another hits right near our trench and sprays water and dirt all over my shirt.

Wolf and I had only thought of battling with dirt and mud. We are entirely unprepared for a water balloon strike, and who knows how many more are in that bag.

Wolf raises his hand straight up, and then turns his wrists back and forth twice in what is probably our most important hand symbol, which means *Let's get out of here, quick!*

Wolf rushes to top of the ladder and rolls to the side on the grass. "Hey!" he calls to me. "Hand me some mud balls."

I send up four big ones that he protects under his body. A huge green balloon lands right on his back and explodes. Wolf lets out a small scream, and then a bunch of laughter.

"Come on, Sergeant Salazar. It's our turn now. Let's go get 'em."

The truth is that no kid in Los Angeles in July can resist the feeling of a water balloon splattered all over them. It's really hot, and the one city pool where we live is too crowded. So once you get over the humiliation of being hit, the cool water is a kind of heaven. But still, we have to get these guys back.

Wolf loves to run. He has long thin legs that don't fill up his pants. I know about the way Wolf's legs look because I am always running behind him, trying to keep up. My legs

are short by comparison, and I run much slower than he does. I breathe in the smog as I run and my lungs feel too tight, slowing me down even more. This could be why I am getting hit by so many more balloons–one, two, three, four direct hits to his one. We're both totally soaked by the time we make it to the other small trench and launch the four mud balls.

Jaime and Diego bend over and try to cover their bodies with their arms while they laugh their heads off. They jump out of their trench to pursue us as we run away. The four of us run and run, following the massive figure-eight bike track, until Wolf, without warning, shouts, "Oh yeah, I'm Steve Sax, stealing home base again for the Dodgers." He slides long into the mud puddle in front of Mrs Vega's house.

This causes a big pileup.

"Well, I'm Pedro Guerrero." Jaime laughs and squeezes his bicep. "And I can hit more home runs than all of you combined."

Wolf reaches under Jaime's flexed arm and begins tickling him. Jaime jerks his body back, trying to defend his armpit and belly, and ends up splashing more of the cool, wet mud on top of us.

"Hey, watch it," I complain.

Diego jumps me and tries to pin himself on top of me.

"What Dodger are you?" he asks, trying unsuccessfully to keep me pinned down and tickle me at the same time.

"Alejandro Peña," I say between giggles.

"Ah, he isn't as good as Fernando," Diego insists.

"He's more fun to watch, though, squeezing his little bag, patting the dirt with his cleats," I answer.

"It's true that you're as slow as him," Diego counters.

"He's just taking his time," I explain. And then I push with all my strength to flip Diego over. "He pitches when he's ready."

I feel a pain in my chest as it hits against Diego's shoulder. It's been hurting ever since school let out last month. I bring my left arm back to protect it from getting bonked again, but this leaves me only one arm to fight with.

Wolf sees me struggling and jumps up and tackles Diego, only to get tackled in turn by Jaime. I wish I wasn't always on the bottom, but I can't grip anything to pull myself up. Everything is slippery and sloshy. Wolf manages to stand up and starts flexing his muscles.

"I am the fastest man alive," he announces with a big grin. "I'm Carl Lewis and I'm going to leave the rest of you in the dust." He starts singing the Olympic music from all the TV commercials at the top of his lungs.

It's so corny that we all crack up before he bounces on top of us again.

I don't feel so mad at Diego today. Throwing mud at each other really makes you feel better. This is what it's like between us. We get into an argument, and then we make competitions or battles, and then it seems better. Fun even. Maybe it's because Diego lives right across from me and that's too close to not get on each other's nerves. Maybe it's because I beat Jaime in math class, and Wolf beats Diego in sports. Maybe it's because no matter how many competitions Wolf and I win, everyone thinks that Jaime and Diego are cool, and that we're kind of dorky.

Diego finally manages to pull himself out of the pile and challenges, "Okay, get ready for round two."

And with that, Diego and Jaime run off back to their trench.

Wolf and I pull ourselves up and look at each other. The mud has plastered our clothes to our bodies. I look down at myself and I can see the two new bumps on my chest sticking out a bit under my slick, muddy shirt. The right bump is bigger than the left. I quickly pull my shirt away from my skin. As I walk back to our trench, I hold my shirt out so it doesn't cling to my chest. I don't want anyone to see my bumps, but walking like this looks weird.

Wolf holds his shirt out, too. "Why are we doing this with our shirts?" he asks.

"It's good to air out," I say.

"Right," he says and pulls his shirt all the way off. He lays it on the grass next to the trench to dry out.

I look at his flat, regular-sized nipples for a second and miss the way mine used to be. I keep my shirt on as I climb back down into the trench. It's wet and kind of miserable, but at least it's dark enough in the trench that Wolf can't see my chest very well.

Anyway, we've already got new incoming rounds of mud and water balloons, so thankfully, there's no more time to think about my stupid bumps. We engage in eight more such battles. Either Diego and Jaime throw their balloons at us until we jump out and run while they chase us, or Wolf and I launch our mud balls at them until they can't take it anymore and jump out and we chase them. After a couple of hours, Wolf and I lie filthy and exhausted at the bottom of our trench. We point our feet at opposite ends so that the tops of our heads rest together in the middle.

15:00.

"We need a good name for it," I say, jotting ideas in my field notebook. Wolf told me I wouldn't have any time in our trench for writing, but unless you write it down, nobody will even know it happened.

"For what?" Wolf asks. He gets to his feet and climbs halfway up the ladder. He starts scanning the street with my binoculars once again.

"For the war," I explain.

"Oh yeah," he says. "We could spend the whole summer at war. It's momentous. We better make it a good one."

"The Sidewalk War?" I suggest.

"Nah, sounds too gentle and nice. Warriors don't use sidewalks," he explains. "How about the Battle of Muscatel?"

"Maybe that's not such a good idea. Muscatel is the name of our street, but my nana said it's also the name of cheap wine. It would be weird to name our war after wine." I shake my head. "Teenagers could show up with the wrong idea."

"Good point," Wolf says. "We don't want that." Then a smile spreads across his face and he proudly rhymes, "Street War of Eighty-Four!"

I nod. "I like it."

chapter 6

LONG ENOUGH

We only stop battling when we see my mom's car round the corner onto our street and wobble slowly through the mud toward us. My mom pulls into the driveway, opens her door, and grabs her stuff from the back seat.

I turn to Wolf and put my finger over my lips, making a silent *Shhhhh*.

We stay hidden and quiet until she goes inside, and then we creep out of our hole in the ground. I know my mom won't be happy with the mountain of mud on my clothes. I take a deep breath and open the front door.

Luckily, my mom is busy looking through the mail, so I motion for Wolf to follow me toward my bedroom. But just when I think we're safely out of sight, my mom says, "Alex?"

"Yeah?" I answer from around the corner.

"Did you put the chicken in the oven?"

"Oh no." I cringe. "I'm sorry, Mom. I forgot."

"It's okay, honey, but you know it means that we need to wait another hour or so before we get to eat."

"I'm okay with that. I'm not hungry yet, anyway," I say, and inch closer to the safety of my bedroom.

"Well, can you put it in now?" she says. "I've got a couple of calls to make."

"Uh, yeah," I say, while Wolf is frantically pointing at the bathroom. I nod at him, understanding. "Oh, um, I just gotta go to the bathroom first."

At that moment, Johnny emerges from his bedroom, looks at us dragging our muddy bodies down the hallway, and starts cackling.

I put my hands together in fake prayer and whisper, "Please, please don't tell," but before he can answer, I hear my mom's loud voice behind us.

"What is going on?! What happened to your clothes?!"

My nana appears behind her and gasps. "There was a collapse in the caves?"

"What caves?" my mom asks.

"The caves in México," I answer quickly. "When she was a little girl, and the armies were bombing–"

"She sought shelter in the caves. Yes, I know. I know that story," my mom says, exasperated. "But what does that have to do with all the mud on your clothes?"

"Um, just a little street war against Diego and Jaime?" I try to say nonchalantly.

"A street war?!" she yells.

"You know, mud and water balloons and stuff like that," I try again.

"And Wolf, too?"

"I'm on Alex's side, Ms Salazar," he answers earnestly. "And I do believe we have the upper hand."

My mom sighs. "All right. Wolf, I'll call your dad to see if you can stay for dinner. In the meantime, both of you get these clothes off and into the washing machine."

I start toward the bathroom, but Wolf doesn't follow.

"You too, Wolf," my mom insists.

"I'm okay, Ms Salazar. I'm used to the mud."

"That may be," she says. "But my house isn't used to the mud."

"Really, I can just brush it off outside," he insists.

"If you want to war around with Alex in the mud this summer," she threatens, "you two are going to have to wash your clothes."

"But I don't have anything else to wear," he pleads.

"Alex, loan him a shirt and pants," my mom says. "Wolf, tomorrow bring two sets of your uniform so that you can be more comfortable, okay?"

"I don't know." Wolf looks down at the crusty mud on his fatigues.

"Look at me." She catches his eye. "We'll get these cleaned before bedtime, and I promise not to tell anyone you ever had them off."

Wolf wears a lot of dirty clothes. He didn't used to. When we were still in school, the girls would fan their noses and say he smelled bad. Wolf pretended not to notice. I don't think his dad knows how to do the laundry, because I'm pretty sure Wolf stopped having clean clothes when his mom died.

Wolf hesitates but hands over his rumpled pile of clothes. I choose my gray corduroys and a blue shirt, and he finds a white T-shirt and jean shorts in my drawers. Wolf looks at himself in the mirror in my bedroom for a moment, and then his shoulders hunch over.

"They fit you perfect," I offer.

"I hate them," he answers.

"Jeez, and that's one of my better T-shirts," I joke. "Only two stains on it."

"Whatever," he says curtly.

For the next couple of hours, Wolf slouches and looks smaller and not as strong as he does when he's wearing his uniform. I try to get him to talk, but he ignores me. I try to cheer him up by sneaking us chocolates after dinner. He eats them but doesn't look any happier. He asks my mom if he can watch television with my nana until he has to go home. Since it's a boring history show, I follow my mom to her bedroom, where she is primed to hang out for the night with one of her mystery novels.

I jump onto the bed next to her, but she looks at me suspiciously over the top of her book. "You're not going to wiggle are you?" she says.

"No, Mom, I promise not to."

"You always promise not to."

"This time I *really* promise not to."

She extends her arm so that I can lay my head across her shoulder and snuggle up. "I know you'll still wiggle," she tells me.

"Yeah," I admit.

She puts her book down and starts moving her fingers through my hair. "What's wrong, mija?" she asks softly.

I didn't really know something was wrong until she asked. "Well, me and Wolf had fun all day ..." I begin, my tummy feeling shaky.

"I could see that from your clothes," she can't resist saying.

I give her a dirty look for not letting me finish before I've barely started. "But anyway, now all of a sudden Wolf won't talk or hang out or anything. Like he's mad at me or something."

"Oh," she says, "I don't think he's mad at you." She moves up on her elbow beside me. "You know, since his mom died–"

"But that was a long time ago," I interrupt, frustrated.

"Two years is actually not a long time when someone dies."

I don't say anything. I want her to take my side, not Wolf's.

"It's probably my fault," my mom says. "I made him take off his uniform. He really didn't want to do that."

"Yeah, but it's just for a couple hours. I've had to wear things that I didn't like before. Like when Dad was still around and you made me wear those dumb dresses to church all day long."

She smooths my hair down. "It's not as hard to wear dumb dresses when you've got your mom with you."

Actually, it is hard to wear dumb dresses, with or without a mom. I'm glad we stopped having to go to church when my dad left. I hated sitting on the church pew in yellow-and-white-flowered laciness. Wolf must feel awful when he doesn't have his uniform. I shouldn't be mad at him. He doesn't have his clothes, or his mom, to protect him.

And then I get scared. I imagine what it would be like if my mom left me, too. I can see myself in a horrible dress at church, alone. I grab her and hold on tight.

"What's wrong?" she says again, startled.

"I don't want you to ever die, not ever," I say, my mouth muffled by her shoulder.

"No, mija. Don't worry."

"I don't want you to ever move away either."

"That's not going to happen."

I lay my head on her big, soft arm.

"But Dad left one day, just like that. And I don't know where he is or why he did that."

"I wish I knew, honey," she answers.

"Maybe he was mad at me for making too many messes around the house or something?" I propose.

"No, honey, no." She looks me straight in the eyes for a moment. "He wasn't upset with you."

I look back into her eyes and try to believe what she's saying. "Well, then, why would he leave?"

She turns away. "I think he was having a hard time ..." Her voice drifts off.

"Like hard how?" I ask.

"You know it upsets me to talk about him, Alex," she cautions. "Can we talk about something else?"

"Well, then, what if *you* have a hard time?"

"Listen to me," she says. "I'm not going anywhere, not for a long, long time."

She reaches out to pet my hair again, but her arm accidentally brushes against my chest.

"Ow," I say.

"Oh," she says. "Did I hurt you?"

"No, no," I lie. "I just scratched my toe against my leg. That's all."

I don't want to tell her about my chest feeling so sore. It's like a hard ball right near my heart, and that can't be good. My nana has always claimed that you can die of a broken heart. I'm betting this much pain so close to my heart could kill me. I don't want my mom to worry about me. She's already too stressed out and tired every night from her job.

She resumes petting my head, and this makes me feel calmer.

Finally, she pulls away a bit. "Maybe things will get a little better for Wolf."

"What do you mean?" I say, so glad for the change of topic.

"Maybe a new member of the household?"

"What do you know?" Any information about Wolf should be told to me right away! He's *my* friend. I have a right to know. I sit up quickly and scrunch my eyebrows together. "Well?"

"Ay, Alex, it's not that big of a deal. Who knows? Maybe nothing will come of it."

"Come on, Mom. What?" I say, exasperated.

"When I called his house tonight a woman answered," she says and smiles. "I know you told me not to intrude, but I just had to ask who she was."

Usually, I don't like my mom getting involved with my friends. She can be so embarrassing! But in this specific case, my rules are suspended because I'm dying to know the answer.

"Oh my God, who is she?" I'm desperate.

"She's Wolf's dad's new girlfriend."

Whoa. "He's in love with someone new?" I'm outraged. "Doesn't he still love Wolf's mom?"

"As you said, it *has* been two years."

"That's not long enough." I've seen what stepmothers do to kids in every single fairy tale. And I can't bear for Wolf to be hurt.

"Alex, do you always have to be so dramatic?" She holds my hand and rubs it softly. "Who knows if they'll stay together? But if they do, maybe Wolf will have more of a home again. That house seems so sad ever since his mom died."

"Yeah, that's kind of true," I say, and reach down and hold her hand. "And maybe he would get more birthday presents? Do new girlfriends buy stuff for kids?"

"Alex," my mom sighs, "the love is what's important."

"Oh, I know, for sure," I agree. "But I think Wolf would be okay with having more gifts to open, too."

chapter 7

THE SECRET
WEAPON

When Diego's dad leaves for work the next morning, Wolf and I are ready and waiting for the arrival of the enemy soldiers. We wait and wait, and wait some more. I check my watch (10:30 a.m.) against the times I've logged in our war journal and conclude that something must be very wrong.

"Psssst. Captain McCann." I try to get his attention. The truth is that even though Wolf looks serious and ready for war with the binoculars to his eyes, he usually ends up daydreaming. I get up, walk over, and yank on his leg.

"Hey!" I startle him. "Sergeant Salazar, what are you doing out of position? What if they start bombing us?"

"I don't think they're coming today. It's pretty late."

"What if it's a trick?" His eyes quickly return to the binoculars, scanning the muddy war zone.

"It's possible, but we could hop back into headquarters pretty quick if we needed to."

We climb out of the trench and lie down on its edges in the hot sun. My eyes are closed, but the insides look bright red. I feel like a lizard, quiet and warm and still.

Wolf nudges his foot against mine, giving me friendly little kicks.

"What?" I say.

"What are we gonna do now?" He's antsy, all dressed up for battle with nobody to fight.

Suddenly, Diego's front door slams. We leap back into the trench, practically falling on top of each other and all our stuff.

Before we can get into position, we hear Diego laughing. "Haha! Scared you!"

"I was not!" Wolf yells back, even though he's still scrambling around in the bottom of the trench. I climb back up the ladder to take a peek at what we're facing.

"You should've seen how fast your bodies flew into the ditch," Diego says. "It was pretty funny." He's wearing swim trunks and strutting over to the dented-up black vw with Tony. The car looks terrible, but Tony's still driving it all over town.

"It's not a ditch," Wolf says, offended. "It's a trench. As deep as the ones they had in World War II. Unlike the little hole you guys got in your yard."

"Well, you enjoy your trench today, Rambo Boy," Diego answers. "I'm off to the park for swim lessons."

"Sure, right," Wolf says. "You're just scared."

"Don't worry," Diego assures us. "You're on tomorrow, bright and early."

They drive off and we're left alone in the muddy street.

"Oh, man. What are we gonna do now," Wolf says, disappointed.

"Time for the secret weapon," I say. "Which can only be used in very desperate circumstances."

"What is it?" Wolf looks up at me with huge eyes.

"My nana. Let's go ask her for a plan. She's always got good ideas."

"Seriously? That's your secret weapon? What can your grandma do?"

Despite Wolf's attempts to crush my faith in my nana, I lead the resistant soldier inside the house and to a spot in front of the TV in the living room. My nana looks up at us in a daze, as if we just walked out of her TV show.

"We're bored," I announce.

"The kitchen needs cleaning," she suggests.

Beside me, I know Wolf is rolling his eyes and thinking *I told you so.*

"No, Nana, I mean something fun." I'm not explaining properly. "You see, we're in the middle of a war outside, and we only get a few hours of rest before we have to go back to battle, so we need to make the most of it and enjoy ourselves right now."

Wolf is shaking his head like I've totally lost my mind.

"Oh," my nana says, sitting up straight. "You're right, Alejandra. You must use this time wisely." Her eyes are focused now. "Have you already hidden your riches and drawn up your maps?"

"No," Wolf and I say in unison.

"But Nana, we don't have any riches," I add.

"Everyone has riches that must be hidden before the enemy arrives," she assures me. When I look into her eyes, they are round and still, and I know she's gone back into one of her stories.

"During the revolution," she begins, "we had to be very careful. My grandfather was a shoemaker, and mi mamá and mis tías helped out in his shop. We were pretty poor, but even in war, people need shoes, soldiers especially. Both the government and the revolutionary soldiers would come to my grandfather's store, because marching all over the desert wears boots out pretty quick."

By now the TV is far away, and we sit down on the floor in front of my nana. Wolf is looking up at her with his mouth half-open and I can tell he's in Chihuahua, in northern México, with my nana.

"The banks were a mess, and every day we didn't know how much the money would be worth. Even if you saved up your coins and bills, the rates changed so often that they might be useless from one day to the next. So we traded a lot. Mi abuelo would fix someone's shoes, and they would pay him with eggs or corn or beans or flour or cheese or milk. If he was making them a whole new pair of boots, we might get a chicken. It was great to be able to eat, but you needed to have something extra put aside, just in case something terrible happened. Back then, there weren't any fancy stocks or bonds or retirement funds for when you got old or hurt. Like when my own nana had to go for surgery in the city and the family had to raise the money for the doctor. The only thing you could save, that never lost its value, was jewelry."

"No offense Doña Salazar," Wolf says, "but I don't really like jewelry."

"Me neither," I add, while pushing my fingers through the long, brown, shaggy carpet.

"Don't you like your sparkling gold cross, Lobito?"

He reaches up and holds it between his fingertips. "Yes, but that's God," he explains, "not jewelry."

"I see." My nana nods. "And the jewelry during the war, it wasn't always jewelry either, it was more like money." She touches the gold hoops in her ears. "Unless you came across something really pretty."

"But how could they calculate how much a necklace or a ring was worth?" Wolf asks skeptically.

"Sometimes the soldiers would pay for their boots with a little silver ring or a gold cross. Sometimes their mothers or wives would bring an earring or a few links of a chain necklace to help them out. My family saved any bit of gold or silver we got from them. When we had enough, we'd trade them in at a jeweler for a gold coin. We had to hide the riches well. There was a lot of stealing then, and if our town was bombed, we had to hide in the church for protection, and then anything could happen to our house."

My nana leans over like she's telling us a secret. "We would go out late at night so the neighbors wouldn't see us. I was the lookout. Mi mamá and mi abuelo would dig a deep hole in the yard and place a little sewn bag of the gold or silver inside the earth."

"Wait, Nana," I interject. "I thought you said it was dangerous to dig up the earth."

"Oh, hmm." She taps her finger on her chin. "It's okay to dig up a little bit. If it's for treasures, then it's all right. Especially if you only use your hands."

"Are those real rules, or did you just make them up now?" I ask.

She waves my question away and turns to Wolf to continue her story. "Mi abuelo would ask mi mamá to draw a careful map showing exactly where we would have to dig later to get the riches back when we needed them. She would make beautiful maps, tracing the shapes of the buildings, the plants, the rocks, the anthills, even the little alcove where the cats would hide–everything. She was good at drawing, even though she had terrible eyes and had to hold the paper right up to her face. Then we'd hide the map in our bible, in the Old Testament, because we didn't know anyone who liked reading the Old Testament."

Her eyes sparkle a little as she tells us the next part. "Sometimes I didn't need the map, though." She grins proudly. "One of my tías taught me how to see the tiny lights that shine above buried treasure."

Now that she has finished her story, she gets up from the couch. "Wait here a moment."

Wolf and I sit with our mouths hanging open, looking at each other.

"Do you think it's true that she can see tiny lights above buried treasure?" he asks. "Would she teach us to see them, too?"

"I don't know. I don't think so." Much as I love my nana's stories, I can never tell which parts are actually true.

We sit up straight when she walks slowly back into the living room. She hands each of us a silver dollar.

"Something to start your savings." She smiles. "Remember to bury deep and draw your maps well."

Wolf and I run to my room, where I dump my marbles out of the small tin box I keep them in. It used to be filled with lemon drop hard candies that my tía Hilaria, my mom's sister, gave me for my birthday. We put our coins together

inside the box. I add my violet cat's-eye marble that I won after six rounds of play over two lunch periods. Wolf pulls a picture of Rambo from his wallet and throws it in. I carefully cut out a photo of Hawkeye from the front page of a TV guide and add it, too. Wolf digs around in his backpack, and then hands over a small figure of a knight wearing a royal-blue tunic with a silver helmet and visor. It's one of his favorite toys. I look up at him to make sure he really wants to bury it, and he nods solemnly.

I write a note that informs whoever finds and opens the tin that *The contents of this box belong to Alex and Wolf. Returnable to 3618 Muscatel Ave. Thank you.*

My mom says people are more willing to do things for you if you're polite.

chapter 8

BLOOD

Once our tin is filled up, Wolf and I head to the garage to search for a shovel. The garage has not been used for a car since I've been alive. One side is Johnny's sound studio, and the other is a giant collection of half-smashed old cardboard boxes filled with glasses, books, records, Christmas decorations, and anything else my mom doesn't want to see in the house anymore. There is also a bunch of wood and equipment that used to belong to my dad. Me and Johnny would get in big trouble if we used Dad's tools when he was around, but my mom hasn't cared what we do in here since he left. You can find all kinds of weird, cool stuff, as long you're willing to dig through spiderwebs.

When I open the garage door the light's already on. Johnny is sitting in the far corner, next to the hole Tony made in the wall. He's holding his bass.

"Get out," he orders.

"You don't own the garage," I say smugly.

"I think I told you to leave," Johnny counters.

"Wowwww." Wolf is looking up at all the posters of women with his mouth hanging open.

"Yuck," I say.

I don't like Wolf looking at Johnny's posters. I don't like any guys looking at women's pictures. Actually, that's the only thing I don't like about Hawkeye Pierce from *M*A*S*H*. He's cool in every way except that he looks at women, which is kind of creepy.

Johnny sees that I'm uncomfortable and laughs. "You're going to look like that too in a few years."

"Gross! Shut up," I tell him.

"Whatever, Alex. You've got girly posters in your room, too," he accuses.

Wolf turns and stares at me. My cheeks get hot.

"Wonder Woman is not a girly poster. She's a warrior," I defend myself. "And besides, Lynda Carter and Linda Ronstadt are both part Mexican, just like us."

Johnny smirks. "If you don't like it, leave."

Wolf looks at the ground and plays with his belt loops. I tug his arm and point to the other side of the garage, which

our store of ammunition and won't have any idea about the treasures down below.

It's so bright and hot outside that the air looks warped where it touches the driveway. I'm thankful for the cool mud between my hands, and let it squirt out around my fingers. I watch Wolf digging with all his strength, but the hole only gets an inch deeper. The earth is hard here, and it will take him a while to dig deep enough. He needs time for the water to seep in and soften the dirt. Time to talk, I decide.

"So your dad's got a new girlfriend?"

Wolf looks up, surprised, and then a moment later he understands. "Your mom told you?"

"Yeah." I'm caught.

"How does she always find out about everything?"

I shake my head. "No idea. That's why I always worry about getting in trouble. Somehow, she always knows."

"Totally."

"Is his girlfriend nice?" I ask.

"Sure, she's nice enough. Sometimes she even cooks dinner and brings a video for us to watch."

"You like her?" I pull out more dirt and wet it.

"I don't know," he says softly, moving the shovel around the edges of the hole. "It freaks me out to see my dad with someone else."

"For sure." I think about my mom. "When my mom got a boyfriend I used to put the TV on really loud to drive him crazy. Remember?"

"Not the same thing." Wolf plunges the shovel hard into the ground.

"I know. I just mean if I was that mad without anyone dying, I bet you're super mad."

Wolf puts down the shovel and starts scooping out the mud with his fingers. "That's part of the problem. I don't feel mad. I don't feel anything."

"Yeah," I say, because I don't know what else to say.

"It's like when my leg falls asleep, and I hit it, but I can't feel it."

This is when I like Wolf best. When he talks to me. The only other person he gives that to is the school counselor.

The grown-ups at school make Wolf go to this blonde lady who is supposed to listen to all his sad feelings about his mom. It is the only thing the school does to him that he likes. Ms McIntyre smiles a lot and wears skirts, sweaters, and short leather boots. She looks into your eyes and asks how you are, and then she waits and listens to the answer. I like to run into her in the hallway because she is kind, but the way she waits and listens for an answer makes me nervous. I always tell her I'm late for something and take off. But Wolf smiles back at her, and he tells me later how pretty she is. Wolf started using the word "feel" after he started talking to her.

He carves deeper into the ground. "It's good, I guess, because she makes my dad happy."

"What about you?" I ask, and start pulling the extra dirt out of the hole.

He pauses and gulps in a bunch of air like he's going to cry. "I'm on my own," he answers coldly. He jabs the shovel back into the ground again and catches the side of my hand, slicing my skin.

I scream when I see the blood pouring out.

"Oh no!" Wolf cries. "Aw, jeez! Alex, I'll get you help right away."

I'm too scared to move. Wolf pulls me up off the ground, tells me to hold my hand above my heart (tips from his soldier survival guides), and runs me inside the house.

"Doña Salazar, Doña Salazar, help!" he calls.

Wolf and my nana bring me to the bathroom. My nana washes my hand, which makes it feel like it's on fire, which makes me scream again. And then we can all see that the cut is not as bad as it looked when it had blood all over it. My nana rubs my hand with a cotton ball and peroxide, which makes my skin fizzle. Then she puts a huge bandage on top of it. Once I see my hand all cleaned up, I'm okay again.

"Let's finish the job," I say to Wolf.

Wolf looks at me anxiously. "You can't even move your fingers."

"Duh, I've got another hand," I say. "And we can't leave a big hole for when my mom gets home."

"You've got a point," he says.

We go back outside and kneel beside the hole again. Wolf pushes the shovel away and digs with his hands instead. I look down inside the hole and see that he's carefully moving his fingers around something in the earth.

"What's in there?" I ask.

"Just roots," Wolf says. "Probably from your dad's rosebush."

"Shoot, I guess we dug too close. Be real careful," I warn.

"I am," he says defensively. But then he pauses. "Hey, sorry about cutting your hand."

"It's okay," I say.

Wolf nods. "I think it's deep enough."

"Let me try." I stick my good hand into the hole and rub it around in the dirt. "Those are tough roots. I don't think we hurt them any." I wrap my fingers around one of them to feel how thick and strong it is. My thumb pushes against something plastic.

"There's some trash in there or something," I say.

"Really?" Wolf perks up. "Like what?"

"I don't know." I shrug. "Probably some dumb kid throwing his Toys "R" Us trash into our yard." The only thing our street is famous for is that it winds into the only Toys "R" Us for miles.

"Can you pull it out?" Wolf asks.

"I'm trying," I say, grasping the plastic between my fingers. "It feels like a bag." I pull a corner free from around the root. "See?"

"I can do it." Wolf pushes his hand in next to mine and grabs at the edge.

"Dig some more around it," I suggest.

Wolf starts rounding out the hole so that we can see more of the plastic bag on either side of the root.

"It's so dirty," I say.

"I think it's a Ziploc," Wolf says.

"What if there's an old sandwich in it or something?" I pull back.

"Eww," Wolf says.

"Touch it and see if it's mushy," I say.

"Gross! No way."

"Some soldier you are, afraid of old sandwiches." I stick my hand in again and push around on top of the bag. "It's just flat, like there're papers in it or something."

"Oh?" Wolf says with excitement. He loves old papers.

Wolf sticks his hand in and holds tight to one of the roots while I wiggle the bag out from underneath it. It's covered in dirt, but I unzip the top and a bright white fancy paper is inside. It has black type, with a golden pyramid seal at the bottom. I read aloud.

"Whoa!" Wolf shouts.

Deed of Ownership

Title Description: Aztlán

Location: The Bronze Continent

This is to certify that the bearer of this document, a person of the sun, "who plants the seeds, waters the fields, and gathers the crops," inherits the land hereby known as Aztlán, recognized as the Southwest United States and Northwest México, a portion of the Bronze Continent.

On this 27th day of May, 1972

GO151

"This must be my nana's," I say, disappointed. "When she went to community college a few years ago, she read a bunch of books about Aztlán."

"They let old ladies go to college?" he asks.

"Yep. She even took classes with my cousin," I say. "He thought it was kind of freaky."

"I think it's cool," Wolf says. "You could study things your whole life."

"My uncle said it was crazy, and that 'she needed school like she needed a hole in her head,'" I say.

"I'm totally gonna do that, take classes even when I'm a little old man." Wolf smiles.

"But you don't like school," I blurt out, confused.

"School doesn't like me," Wolf counters.

I peer up at him, confused.

"Anyway, the school therapist swears that I'll do a lot better once I get to college."

I begin to fold up the Aztlán deed to put it away, but Wolf grabs for it.

"Hey, be careful," I caution him. "Don't get it dirty."

"Aztlán's the place your nana talks about, right?" he says. "From when she came to the United States."

"Maybe she somehow put it there for us to find," I say.

"But how could she have dug this big hole?" Wolf says. "And when? It's for sure been down there a while."

I hear the engine first, and then the rumble of my mom's tires pulling up into the driveway.

"Quick!" I shout. "Fill in the hole!"

Wolf and I madly attempt to fill in the hole, but it's too late. First, my mom sees a chunk of her yard destroyed and, a second later, the bandage on my hand.

"I better go," Wolf says, getting up and shaking the dirt off his pants. "Ask your nana about the deed."

He waves and runs off before my mom can cross the yard.

chapter 9

I REMEMBER YOUR STORIES

"I remember specifically telling you not to listen to your nana's dramatic stories because then you could get yourself hurt." My mom is rubbing my shoulders, then pacing, then rubbing again, then pacing. "And what did you do to the front yard? There's a big pile of mud next to the rosebush where there used to be grass! Why would you need more mud when you've got a whole street full of it?!"

"I don't know."

"You could've cut into the roots of the roses. Didn't you notice them right in front of you?" She throws up her arms.

"The sun was shining in my eyes?" I offer.

Johnny laughs loudly at my pathetic attempt at an excuse as he walks by us from the kitchen, a bag of chips in his hand.

"That doesn't help," my mom snaps at him.

"Oh, that's fair," he snarks. "She wrecks your precious yard, but you still find a way to yell at me."

"I didn't yell!" she yells.

He shifts his head so that his long dark hair covers most of his face. "Whatever," he says and disappears into his bedroom.

"Ugh." My mom shakes her head and turns her attention back to me. She examines my bandaged hand. "Why isn't Wolf more careful with you? Just because he's a soldier doesn't mean you are."

"I'm just as tough as he is," I argue. "Just because I'm a girl doesn't mean I can't be a soldier."

"That's true." She nods. "But you could be a girl who gets a PhD instead."

"That sounds totally boring." I groan. "Anyway, it was an accident."

"Baby, don't you understand? Your hands are precious. You write with your hands. You draw with your hands. You cook with your hands. You can't risk hurting your hands."

"I know, I know. I'm sorry. I'll be more careful." Jeez, if she's this upset about a cut on my hand, what'll she do when she finds out that I've got big sore spots growing next to my heart?

My mom gets me some juice and crackers, and Hops the Kangaroo, and sits me in front of the TV next to my nana to heal. When Johnny comes by on his way to the kitchen again, he sees my nice little setup. I smirk and stick my tongue out at him. He gives me a devilish grin and a contorted stinky face in return.

As soon as I hear my mom leave for her Hispanic Professional Women's Association meeting, I try to talk to my nana, but she's watching *Magnum, P.I.* She loves that guy. "He's got a mustache like Pancho Villa's," she likes to tell me. I'd rather watch *M*A*S*H*.

"I think I found something that belongs to you," I say.

"Wait, mija. He just found a new clue about the killer," she says, hunched forward, staring at the TV.

"But this is important," I tell her.

"I knew it!" she exclaims, triumphant. "I did not trust that plumber."

I try again. "Wolf and I found a deed."

A commercial finally comes on. "What kind of deed?" she asks.

"A deed to Aztlán."

My nana laughs. "That's impossible. Nobody owns Aztlán."

"I've got it right here," I say defensively.

She pulls on her reading glasses from the cord around her neck and takes a look at the letter. "Ahh, what a beautiful golden pyramid," she says, her tone full of admiration. "And the words," she says. "The seeds and fields and crops. They come from the Chicano Movement."

"What's a Chicano movement?" I ask.

"Oh!" she gasps. "I forgot to tell you about the Chicano Movement? That's terrible. I'm forgetting too many things, mjia."

"Don't worry, Nana." I reach to hold her hand. "I remember most of your stories, so that means we've got them safe in both of our heads."

She smiles. "You're a good kid."

I get embarrassed when grown-ups compliment me, so I change the subject as fast as possible. "What about the Chicano Movement, Nana?"

"Oh yeah." She takes a sip of her tea, turns down the volume on the TV, and begins. "Mira, way back in the 1840s, when the gringos stole a bunch of México, they made a whole lot of promises to us. They said we would keep our liberty and property rights. But they didn't follow their own rules."

"Like how?"

"You know Dodger Stadium, right?"

"Yeah, of course," I answer. "I love Dodger Stadium."

"Well, that used to be Chavez Ravine, which was stolen from Mexican Americans." She shakes her head sadly. "Your grandpa was so mad about that he resigned from his job with the city."

"Wow," I say. "I didn't know that."

"And Rosemead is full of Mexican kids, but how much Spanish have you learned at your school so far?" she asks.

"None, Nana," I admit. "I've only learned a few words from you."

"We had a right to our language, but they don't give us the chance to learn it." She sounds angry now.

"That's true." I feel sheepish. I wish I knew Spanish better so my nana wouldn't have to be so upset.

"Bueno," she resumes, "we started getting really mad that the gringos weren't keeping their promises. And also that they could be really mean to us, saying racist words and even beating us up sometimes, kicking us out of school, not paying us enough money at work, deporting us, a thousand kinds of awful things."

I lower my head. I feel kind of ashamed of the stories she's telling. Even though I'm part Mexican, I'm also quite a bit American. It's like one part of my body was mean to the other.

She sees my head down and says, "Don't worry, mija, we're just getting to the good stuff."

"There's good stuff?" I ask.

"About twenty years ago, a whole bunch of Mexican Americans started fighting back, marching on the streets, striking in the fields, and demanding better schools and jobs and all the rights we deserve. Some of the ones who were fighting for justice even wore uniforms and called themselves the Brown Berets. In East LA they put together free health clinics for Chicanos, and one of the leaders, Gloria Arellanes, graduated from El Monte High."

"Did anyone from Rosemead ever do anything?"

"Pues, sí." My nana nods proudly. "Vikki Carr, the smoothest Chicana voice on the radio. She's ours."

"Oh," I say. "Is she from the house where the Cardonas live? The one you always point out?"

"That's right." My nana smiles. "I didn't know you were paying attention."

I roll my eyes at her.

She continues. "And all these fighters, all together, named themselves Chicanos and Chicanas," she says triumphantly. "And that is our Chicano Movement."

"But how did the Chicanos take charge of Aztlán?"

"No, honey, Aztlán belongs to the Aztécs, and the Aztécs belong to Aztlán. The Chicanos just feel safer here than anywhere else."

"Because the Aztécs are nicer to them than the Americans?"

She taps on her mug. "Hmm, I doubt they would be. They weren't always so nice to others way back when they were in charge of México before the Spanish showed up."

"Oh, man." I groan. "Well, where is it anyway? Is Aztlán here? Like under our house?"

"Not really. The land under our house would be part of the traditional territory of the Tongva people."

"I'm so confused, Nana," I say impatiently. "Please just tell me where I can find Aztlán and why Chicanos feel safer there?"

My nana pushes her pointer finger first against her temple and then slowly moves it down over her heart. "Aztlán is the land we make in our dreams, mija. It's the sanctuary we escape to when the United States tries to hurt us."

"So it's not actually real!" I am so frustrated.

"It's very real, mija," she corrects me. "But there's no deed for it."

"Did you bury this paper for me to find just so you could tell me all these stories?"

"Oh, that's such a great idea!" she exclaims. "But no."

"Did you bury this for me to find, and then forget that you buried it for me to find?" I try again.

"No," she says confidently. Then less confidently, "I don't think so. Hmm."

"Why would it be buried in our yard?"

"I don't know, mija," she says as she turns the volume back up on her show. "But I gotta at least catch the ending of *Magnum* because he's chasing after that man in the coveralls."

"He always catches the bad guy."

"Yes, and it's very satisfying to watch him do it." She grins.

I keep waiting for a better answer.

"Have you drawn up your map yet?" my nana asks. "Better make it before you forget where you've buried your treasure."

"Okay," I say, and I decide to stop bothering her.

I go to my bedroom and slip the deed into my dresser. I grab my notebook and start working on the map. Holding my hurt hand carefully above the paper, I draw the outlines of all the important landmarks: the rosebush that me and my nana saved from the machines; the long wavy leaves of the bushes that Wolf and I lie under when the days are too hot; the stones that make up the walkway; the metal circle that holds the hose Wolf and I use to fill the mud buckets; the bricks that separate the ferns from the grass; the drive-way that hosted the yard sale Wolf and I set up last year; the patch of dirt that Wolf and I use to pack our mud balls; the maple tree that drops sticky sap on our heads. When I finish drawing with my pencil, I fill in all the images with my watercolors, and then I lay the map out on my desk to dry.

Who does the deed belong to? Why would they bury it in our yard?

What did Wolf mean when he said he was on his own? He's with me. My map would be dumb without Wolf in it.

I go get my nana to show her my work. Her show is finished, so she is happy to come.

She gasps when she sees my bandage. "What happened to your hand, Alex?"

"Wolf accidentally hurt me with a shovel." I try to calm her. "But you patched me up."

"I did?" she asks.

"Yep."

"That's good," she says and looks down at my map. "Ay, qué bonita." She gasps. "The roses look so beautiful."

"Thanks, Nana," I say, and point to an *X* beside them. "That's where we buried our box, and where we found the deed."

"Oh, yes, so important to keep a record," she says. "We used to bury our gold when we lived in México. My abuelo was a shoemaker and would receive eggs, corn, cheese, beans, and all kinds of things in trade for his work. He'd save the bits of gold and silver, and our family would sneak out together and bury it in the night." She smiles. "I was the lookout so that the neighbors wouldn't know where it was buried, because there was a lot of stealing during the war."

She is repeating her story of México once more, but at least she remembers it, even if she doesn't remember saying it. "Was it exciting?"

"I loved getting to stay up late." She retells everything she said in the morning.

I'm happy she thinks my map is beautiful. I must've done it right if it made her think of México. But I'm a little sad, too, that she doesn't remember telling me her stories earlier.

She doesn't remember why the street is full of mud, either. She's been staring at the street and frowning ever since the machines tore it up. Almost every day she asks, "Why are they doing that to the street?" and shakes her head. "Don't they know it's dangerous to dig up the earth?"

"They're putting in sidewalks," I tell her every time.

"Oh," she says, nodding. "Well, that'll be great. You'll be able to roller-skate. When I was a little girl ..."

And then she always tells me the story of being a little girl who roller-skated down the sidewalks of San Francisco to the library at the Civic Center.

At first I used to get mad at her when she would tell me a story over again for the seventeenth time. Now I expect her to repeat herself, and then I'm not surprised when she does. It's much better this way. I actually get more worried when she forgets to repeat her stories.

It's not really that bad. If I'm excited about something at school, or at soccer practice, or with Wolf, I can tell her over and over again and she's surprised each time. She never gets bored of my stories. Most people will hardly listen once. So I feel pretty lucky. The only thing that's confusing is I never know what she'll remember and what she won't.

My nana yawns. "I'm tired, honey. I think I'll go to bed now."

"Good night, Nana."

"Sueña color de rosa," she tells me. She thinks dreaming in the color pink gives people the best sleep.

I smile. "I will."

As she's walking out of my room, she says, "Wolf will be very happy with how well you made your map."

chapter 10

THE SWAP MEET

The next morning is Saturday, which is a big deal during the school year, but during the summer it just means my mom's home. This could lead to a day of shopping or cleaning the house, neither of which are very fun. The only good thing about shopping at the mall is that my mom will buy us corn dogs and lemonades if I make it through all the aisles of the store without complaining too much. The other amazing thing about my mom is that she lets me sleep as long as I want. She hides in her room reading mysteries until I come find her. Every single other kid I know is forced out of bed in the morning, even on weekends. I hold on to Hops and sleep until I have dreams about turning into a dog and racing the other dogs around the neighborhood, or about eating vanilla ice cream with too much butterscotch sauce spilling all over me. I wake up and blink and rub my eyes and lie in bed until I can't stand being in my room one more minute.

That's the kind of morning I was looking forward to, but instead, there is a tapping on my window at seven a.m. When I turn over I can see Wolf's proudly smiling face. He is holding his entire body up in the air by hanging onto my window frame.

Not even my best friend should wake me up early on a Saturday. I turn over.

Wolf whistles four sounds like a mourning dove. It's one of our secret birdcalls, and he knows it's my favorite. But I don't care. My eyes just want to be closed.

He knocks on the window again, a little louder.

Oh, man. Yesterday he cut my hand and today he's ruined my Saturday sleep-in.

After he knocks a third time, there is loud thumping on the other side of my bedroom wall, a warning from Johnny that I better stop Wolf or he's gonna come punch me. No one better ever mess with Johnny's sleep.

Okay, then. I look up at Wolf and point for him to meet me at the front door. I pull on my soccer shorts and go open the front door. Holding my finger over my lips, I say, "Shhhh. Everyone's still asleep."

Wolf's eyes are wide. He whispers, "Does that deed belong to your nana? Does she own Aztlán?"

"Argh!" I say. "Did you wake me up for that?"

"Well, you gotta admit, it would be pretty cool if she did."

I put my hands on my head and moan. "Turns out nobody owns Aztlán, except maybe the Aztécs, but they mostly belong to it."

"What does that mean? To belong to it?"

"I don't know." I shrug.

"But what about the certificate with the gold seal?"

"It's not hers. But she said it's got Chicano words."

"What does that mean?"

"Well, Chicanos are Mexicans living in America, like my mom's family. They used to march for more rights and stuff when we were babies, like Black people, like Martin Luther King Jr.," I explain. "Probably not in Rosemead, but maybe in El Monte, or for sure East LA."

"Oh," Wolf says. "Did they have uniforms?"

"Some of them had brown ones," I offer.

"Huh," he says. "They never talked about that in school."

"Yeah, that's true. I only know from my nana."

"There were soldiers marching right here in the San Gabriel Valley when we were babies, and nobody ever told me?" Wolf says, annoyed. "I'm going to have to look this up at the library."

"It's not even open yet," I say. "You're going to study on a Saturday?"

"Sure, why not?" Wolf says. "But anyway, we've got other business first. I'm taking you to the swap meet."

"Why do we need to go to the swap meet?" I ask. It's shopping, and shopping is boring. Plus, it's clear over on the other side of the city. "It's so far."

"You need a uniform," he announces.

"What do you mean? What's wrong with my soccer shorts?" I hold them out and look down at myself.

"They're fine for school," Wolf explains. "But we're at war this summer. And we're in the same army. We can't look disorganized."

I have to admit, it does sound kind of cool to get a uniform. I've never had one before. I've never seen one at Montgomery Ward's department store. Definitely not in the girls' section. "But it'll take so long to get there."

"Not if we go in the wash. It makes a diagonal that goes straight there. I tried it out last week."

"It's against the law to be in the wash. And you're already in trouble with the police," I remind him.

"I finished those dumb anger management classes they forced me to take." He smiles. "And besides, nobody's gonna see us."

The purpose of the wash is to gather up extra water if it rains hard, but most of the time it's just got a dribble full of green algae running down the middle. You're not supposed to go down there. Only workers are allowed. But teenagers do it. They light firecrackers to hear the echoes bounce off the concrete. There are ladders under each overpass if you need to make an escape, but you could basically get trapped and die in a ten-foot-deep cement canal if there was a flash flood. It's not a good idea. They once found a dead teenager down in the wash, some guy who was in my brother's class.

"My mom says it's very dangerous, especially if it rains."

Wolf shakes his head. "It hasn't rained in a year. It's not going to start today. It's summertime and the sun is already shining."

"Can we get back by noon? My mom won't expect me to be up until then." I scrunch my hair with my hand. "'Cause if she finds out, I'll be in big trouble."

Wolf and I quietly scour the house, looking under couch cushions, along the floor, and behind the washing machine, collecting any coins we find. Between us we have $7.35.

He nods at me. "It's enough." And we head out.

It's scary climbing over the chain-link fence and into the wash. I don't like being so high up off the ground. The top of the fence is six feet up from the street, and then it's another ten feet to the bottom of the wash. That's way too high, so I close my eyes as I sling my other leg over. I would die if I fell to the concrete bottom.

My nana told me that the wash used to be a regular river. When there was enough water, she would pack a picnic and my grandpa would fish when they were first together. When there was too much water, it would flood across the whole city. That was a long time ago, before the workers came and poured cement on top of all the water and dirt and animals. I hope they never finish building our street because I don't want all that cement on top of everything.

Wolf and I walk and run and yell in the wash all the way to the swap meet. He was right. This was a good idea. Nobody can see us here. It's like we're invisible. It's like we're spies. It's like our trench back on the street, private and for us only, but full of cooling breezes and graffiti. Wolf thinks we could walk all the way across Los Angeles without anybody noticing, but I'm happy to climb up near the swap meet. I'm out of breath because I can never keep up with his long legs.

Now I understand where Wolf gets all his army clothes. A big parking lot is covered with rows and rows of people and the stuff they're selling. At the end of the second aisle is an old man with a big stomach sitting behind a white plastic table. The table is piled high with green shirts and pants and belts and buckles, with tall black boots lined up along the ground.

He smiles at Wolf. "Have you been practicing your whistling?"

Wolf whistles his mourning dove sounds again.

"Wow, that's real good," the man says. And then his voice gets serious. "Are you low on supplies?"

"Yes, sir," Wolf answers, like the man's his commanding officer. "Alex, here, is in my unit, and we're fighting over on Muscatel. Could go on for a couple of months."

The old man nods. "He need a uniform?"

"Yes, sir," Wolf replies, and the two of them start digging through the stacks.

Mostly when I go out places people think I'm a boy. Johnny says it's because of my short hair and the way I walk

like a cowboy. He laughs when it happens, and I get embarrassed. He doesn't laugh when people mistake him for a girl because of his long hair. I like it better when I'm with Wolf because he doesn't say anything. He doesn't try to tell anyone I'm a girl, and I don't either, and then it doesn't matter. I could be a boy all day long with Wolf and it's fine.

Wolf presents me with size small green camouflage army pants. They're made of thick cotton, and they're full of pockets and buttons. And they're brand new. I never get to have brand-new boys' clothes. My mom lets me wear my brother's hand-me-downs because it saves money, but shopping is only for new girls' clothes. Girls' clothes always have a ruffle or a flower or a lacy thing on them that makes me feel like crying. But this old man, he doesn't even sell girls' clothes. The pants are only five dollars and he throws in a green T-shirt for two dollars. He folds my new uniform up in a brown paper bag and puts it in my hands. This is all mine.

Once we get back into the wash, Wolf says, "Hey, you could put the uniform on. Nobody's down here."

But I'm embarrassed to change in front of Wolf. I don't want him to see how my chest is growing. "Nah," I say. "I want to wait 'til Monday so it'll be fresh for battle."

"Oh, okay," he answers, and then pauses. "Alex, I'm still thinking about the deed. Even if it's Chicano words, it's still gotta belong to someone."

"It's probably my nana's," I say. "I bet she just forgot she buried it."

"Can we take it to the library?" Wolf asks. "The librarians usually know things."

"Is the library even open during the summer?" I wonder.

"Uh-huh," he responds, like it's obvious.

"But why do people need it if they're not doing homework?" I'm baffled.

"To find out stuff. And, well, probably, the free air-conditioning," he concedes.

"I'm not sure," I say. "My mom might want me to help her do housework or something."

"I bet you she'd totally let you go if you told her you were going to the library."

"That's probably true." So much for my plan for a summer without books.

We make our way back to my house through the wash. Whenever we see a big clump of something beside the algae, I turn my eyes away in case it's something dead. We walk fast and kick rocks that ricochet loudly off the concrete walls.

chapter 11

HE DOESN'T WANT TO

Wolf and I sit in the library, looking into the screen of a large machine that magnifies old newspapers.

"I thought only grown-ups got to use these machines," I remark.

"Nope," Wolf says. "It's a public library, and we're the public."

I wonder why Wolf likes the library but hates school. He reads everything but still gets bad grades. He fights back if the teachers tell him what to do but doesn't mind if the librarians shush him. Maybe he likes the quiet. He talks to me a lot when it's just the two of us, but he doesn't really say much when there's a bunch of kids around.

"Okay, I gotta admit this place is cooler than I thought," I say.

If you push the button on the machine, it whips a strip of film around really fast. Zoooooom. It's totally fun.

"Please don't play with the equipment," warns the tall librarian with the big orange hairdo.

"Yes, ma'am," Wolf says in his most polite voice. But then he grins at me and starts zooming it again.

"It says go to N8 for Aztlán," I direct him.

Wolf slows the film and lands on August 29, 1970. The photos show giant crowds. There are kids and grown-ups with their fists in the air. They have placards with La Virgen de Guadalupe and black eagles and peace signs, with "CHICANO POWER!" and "CHILDREN of AZTLÁN" and "OUR FIGHT IS AT HOME NOT IN VIETNAM" written across them. The newspaper article says, "Protesters demand an end to the war in Vietnam, an end to racism in the schools, an end to police brutality. They want immigration reform, better conditions for workers. They are calling for Chicano liberation."

"Wow, they had over twenty thousand people marching!" Wolf exclaims.

"Please keep your voices down," says an old man from the other side of the bookshelves.

"The police shot tear gas canisters into the crowd and killed three Mexican Americans, including *Los Angeles Times* journalist Ruben Salazar," I read.

"Salazar?" Wolf says. "Is that one of your relatives?"

"Nah," I answer. "I think someone would've told me. But it's creepy anyway."

"Please. Keep your voices down," the orange-hairdo librarian warns.

"Why would the police kill them?" I whisper.

"Police can do awful things to you if they don't like you," Wolf says.

I look at Wolf's sad eyes and think of the police taking him away from school in their squad car that day last year. I wonder what they said to him.

I look back at the screen and study the photograph. "That street looks like it's right here, like it's Valley Boulevard. It looks like someone is getting killed on Valley Boulevard."

"But it says it's on Whittier Boulevard in East Los Angeles," Wolf corrects. "I would guess it's around ten miles away."

"It's still scary," I say.

"Yeah," he agrees. "But sometimes you have to fight, and sometimes soldiers get killed."

"But look, they were fighting against being soldiers," I say sadly.

"Rambo would never do that," he says.

"Hawkeye would," I retort.

"There's nothing really here about Aztlán," he says, changing the subject.

"Don't worry about it," I say. "Maybe my nana got the deed at the community college or something." I lay my head down on the wide cool desk.

"Can I borrow it?" he asks. "I can go ask the librarian if she knows anything about it."

"Sure, okay," I say. "Wait. You can just ask librarians about anything?"

"Yep," he says.

"Wow." I've definitely got a question.

While Wolf goes off to speak with the orange-hairdo librarian, I go as quickly as possible to the other side of the library.

I stand in front of a librarian who's sitting behind a tall desk. She is busy flipping through a card catalog. There are flyers advertising tickets for the Olympics, with colorful rings and a gymnast holding herself above a bar. I frown. My mom took me and Johnny to one of the Olympic soccer games, but she says it's too expensive to go to events inside like gymnastics. I take a flyer anyway and stick it in my pocket.

"How can I help you?" says the short, dark-haired librarian with a nice smile.

I look down at the shiny tiles on the floor. "Do you have any medical books?" I ask softly.

"Certainly," she responds. "What type of medicine are you interested in?"

"Um ..." I hesitate. "Like about hearts, or heart attacks, or heart sores?"

"Heart sores?" she asks.

"You know"–I point timidly to my swollen chest–"like a sore over your heart."

Her confused frown changes into a big "Ohhh." She nods. "Yes, I believe we do have some material about heart sores."

"Oh, that's so great!" I say, and then whisper, "Can I check the book out, but like, kind of quietly?"

"Quietly?"

"I don't want my friend to see it," I say. "I don't want him to worry unless it's something serious."

"Ahh, right," she says. "There's no need to worry him. Let me take your information, and then you can just come by for the book on your way out."

"Wow. That would be so great. Thank you." I smile.

I find Wolf back at the microfilm machine, reading more 1970s newspapers.

"Did the librarian know anything about the deed?" I ask.

"She's checking on it and will let me know if she finds anything," he says.

"Oh. What'll we do while we wait?"

"Remember all the times we used to have to wait forever when our parents were filling up at the gas station?" he asks, unable to take his eyes off the screen.

"Yeah," I answer. It used to get so hot in the long lines of cars, sitting in the back seat of our old station wagon. I felt like I couldn't breathe. I hated it.

"It was because of Iran," he says, nodding confidently.

"Weren't they the ones who kidnapped all those Americans? And then they all got off the airplane on TV?"

"Yep, that's Iran," he confirms.

"Oh, okay," I say. I'm not really sure where Iran is. I'm not really interested in facts about gasoline and countries far away. I don't know why he is telling me this stuff. "Is there just old newspapers on this machine, or other stuff, too?"

"Oh, there's tons of stuff. Newspapers, magazines, phone books," he says with excitement, zipping the film back up into the reel. "What do you want to look for?"

"Wait. Did you say phone books?" My heart pounds.

"Yeah," Wolf says. We look into each other's eyes, and he sees what I'm thinking. "Oh. I get it."

"Maybe we can find him," I say.

"Let's try." He opens a small metal drawer full of film strips. "What's your dad's full name?"

"Charles Edmund Richardson."

"Okay, should we start east or west?"

"East," I say. "He always liked valleys more than the ocean."

We zip through the film feeds of the cities to the east of us: El Monte, Diamond Bar, Covina, West Covina, Azusa, Chino, Ontario, Pomona, Rancho Cucamonga. A few Richardsons, but no C., no Charles. We go to the west: San Gabriel, East LA, Alhambra, Pasadena, Monterey Park, Huntington Park, Glendale, Burbank. We go south: Montebello, Pico Rivera, Whittier, South Gate, Downey.

"There's a C. Richardson in Downey," Wolf announces.

My heart thumps. "Oh, wow!" I can't believe it. "That could be him." I copy down the address and phone number. "My mom will be so surprised!"

"If it's actually him," Wolf cautions.

"I'm so happy!" I exclaim.

"Shhhhh." An old lady nearby gives me an evil glare.

I whisper to Wolf, "I'm so excited."

He smiles.

"I gotta go to the bathroom," I say. "And then can we get out of here?"

"I'll check on the deed," Wolf says.

I sneak back over to the nice librarian, who has my medical book ready to go. When she sees me, she nods and pulls out a folded brown paper bag with a book inside.

"Thank you," I say, and head over to the bathroom.

I enter the little hallway to the bathrooms, and I'm just about to open the door to the girls' bathroom when I hear a loud voice behind me.

"Where do you think you're going?" booms the orange-hairdo librarian. "That is the ladies' room."

Her loud voice is jarring in the quiet library. It shakes me.

I turn around. "Um," I say. I am not sure whether to tell her I'm a girl or go to the boys' washroom. I'm not sure which one will make me less in trouble.

She spots the bag in my hand with the library book and grunts, "Books are not permitted in the bathrooms."

"Oh, uh." I'm in more trouble.

I look up at her face. Her lips are pursed and her forehead is wrinkled. Maybe I shouldn't try to go to the bathroom at all. I could make it the ten-minute walk home if we leave soon. But if Wolf starts running, I could end up peeing myself. The orange-hairdo librarian is standing between me and the exit, and I don't know how to get past her body. I look back down at my tennis shoes, dirty from our muddy street.

"It's okay, Helen." I hear the other librarian's firm voice. "*She* has already checked out that book."

The orange-hairdo librarian takes a long look at me, up and down my body, shakes her head, and leaves.

Thank you, I mouth at my nice librarian.

She nods, her lips dropping slightly. Her eyes look soft.

I go to the bathroom quickly, stash my book in my backpack, grab Wolf, and head for the door.

We hit the July sun, and for a second, I forget how to breathe. Hot air must be as good as cold air for breathing, but it doesn't feel that way. It's full of smog, and it hurts if you fill your lungs all the way up. This doesn't stop us from half walking, half running back to my house, though.

"Guess what?" Wolf says with excitement.

I am thankful that he has something to talk about, because I do not want to think, or talk, about the bathroom. "What?"

"She found the artist," he says.

"What artist?"

"An artist made that deed." He smiles. "Actually, he made two hundred of them, and we've got number one hundred and fifty-one."

"Wow," I say. "What artist?"

"Gustavo Ortíz. G-O!" he exclaims. "That's why it says GO151 in the bottom corner."

"No way!" I say. "I didn't notice that."

Gustavo Ortíz. Chicano artist and muralist. Important works: a portrait series of members of the Brown Berets in East LA. Those were the Chicano soldiers my nana told me about.

"We should look for his phone number, too," I say. "Maybe he can tell us why it's buried in the yard."

Wolf frowns. "We can't."

"Why not?" I ask.

"He died of AIDS in January," he says quietly. "Nineteen forty to nineteen eighty-four."

"Wow, that's sad," I say. "That's not very old."

"Yeah," Wolf agrees.

When we walk by some kumquat trees, Wolf hoists himself onto the fence next to them and picks a couple off the branches for us. We suck on the tangy fruit until we reach the corner.

I look over at Wolf. "I think I want to be alone to ask my mom about my dad's phone number," I say.

"I get it," he answers. "Good luck. See you Monday."

When I get home my nana is setting my mom's perm in the kitchen. One of her proudest possessions is her 1931 Hollywood beauty school certificate. She claims that cutting people's hair got her through the Great Depression. She forgets all kinds of things, but she doesn't forget how to style hair.

My mom is sitting on a stool, reading one of her mystery novels. She doesn't look happy to be trapped there with my nana, but she's told me before that she likes the price of a home permanent.

"Mom, you'll never guess what I found at the library!" I shout.

"A book?" she says sarcastically.

"No."

"You didn't find a book to read at the library?"

"There were plenty of books."

"Did you skate to the library?" my nana asks. "I used to love to skate to the library when I was a little girl."

"No, I just walked, Nana."

"What about a magazine?"

"No, Mom, stop. Listen." I'm getting frustrated.

"Okay. Tell me." She smiles. "What did you find at the library?"

I sit down next to her stool and dig around in my backpack, looking for the little paper with the name on it. It's probably squished underneath my book. I pull out the deed to Aztlán and put it on the floor beside me. I feel the corner of the little paper under the book and tug. I look up again at my mom.

She stares down at the deed and speaks very calmly. "They had that at the library?"

"No, no, that's not it," I say. "I found that buried in the yard."

"Buried? Where?"

"By the rosebush," I say. "But that's not what I'm trying to tell you!" I am exasperated.

"Lift your head up, mija. I've got to trim the top." My nana nudges my mom's chin and snips at her hair.

I look at my little piece of paper and read, "C. Richardson, 10805 Myrtle Street, Downey, 555-2182."

"Where did you find that?" my mom asks in the same calm voice.

"It's gotta be Dad, right?!" I exclaim. "It was amazing! The library had phone books from everywhere, and I found Dad inside one of them!"

"You found Charlie," my nana says. "That's so wonderful. Did he come home from the party?"

"What party?" I say.

"C. Richardson could be a lot of different people, Alex," my mom says.

"He was out too late," my nana explains, as she twirls my mom's hair onto rollers.

"Who was out too late?" I ask.

"It's probably not him," my mom declares.

"We used to go out really late during the war," my nana says.

I'm so confused. I answer my nana, "Because you had to look for the buried gold."

She nods and smiles. "If we didn't draw the maps well, we would be out there half the night digging."

I turn to my mom. "But we've got this number, so we could just call it and find out if it's him or not." I run to the white-painted phone and start to dial. "Is Downey in our new area code or the old one?"

"I don't know," my mom answers, irritation in her voice.

"It's okay," I say. "I'll just try both."

"Hang up the phone, Alex!" my mom shouts in her emergency voice.

I drop the receiver fast, like I picked up a burning pot handle. I turn and look at my mom. Her eyes are big and red. "Why?" I say softly.

She knocks the bits of hair off the apron she's wearing and unsnaps the neck. She stands up and speaks in a really slow voice. "Your dad knows where we live, Alex."

"Yeah, but now we know where he lives," I say in a hopeful voice.

"You need to listen now, Alex." She looks into my eyes. "He can find us easily, anytime he wants to." She pauses. "He doesn't want to."

I feel like someone hit me. Tears fall out of my eyes, and I think I might barf. "You don't know that!" I cry. "I could tell him that I'm older now and not as messy in the house or picky with my food. And then he'd like it better."

"Alex, honey." She reaches her hand out to me, but I turn my head away from her.

"Mija," my nana says to my mom, interrupting us, "he might come home if you lost some weight and found a pretty outfit."

"Not now!" my mom shouts at her.

My nana looks confused and shakes her head. She turns to me. "Your mother has always been a bit emotional."

Johnny suddenly walks in with his hand pushed down into a big box of cereal. He scoops up a bunch and throws it into his mouth.

We all stare at him.

"What?" he says defensively. "If I eat out of the box, I don't need to wash a bowl."

chapter 12

THE STREET
BELONGS TO US

Monday morning. 08:52.

My mom has gone off to work, and Wolf and I can resume our battle. I want to go out there early and start my watch from the trench.

"La soldadera!" my nana exclaims with delight when I walk into the kitchen wearing my uniform.

I smile because, even though I'm still mad that my mom won't let me call my dad, I can't help but feel happy in my new clothes.

"Have I told you before about my tía Alicia in Chihuahua?" My nana's eyes shine.

Of course she has. "She's my favorite," I say. "She cut her hair, stole your abuelo's suit, and signed up to fight for the revolution."

"With Pancho Villa!" My nana is still so proud, even though that was a long time ago.

"That must have been exciting," I say. "She got to be a real live warrior."

"Pues, sí. Alicia was excited and so was my mother. But not my tío Ernesto, because he was her big brother and didn't think a woman should carry a gun." My nana takes a sip of her coffee and launches into the story.

"Alicia was one of those kids who always got bored at home, in the kitchen, in my abuelo's shoe shop, everywhere. She couldn't sit still. She wouldn't take the time to sew the leather on the boots, and her littlest sister, my tía Lupe, would have to finish them, or mi abuelo would be disappointed in everyone."

"Lupe used to pinch Alicia to get back at her, but Alicia would stare right at her sister and say, 'You can't make me cry.'" My nana shakes her head. "Tía Alicia would say, 'I was born to *wear* soldier's boots, not waste my time fixing up other people's boots.'"

My nana's eyes fill with tears. "She wore them, but she died in the first battle right outside our town." She shakes her head again. "I don't think she was born for that."

I hug my crying nana. It's not fair that she has to feel every sad thing in her whole life over and over again.

"Cuidado, mija," she whispers to me. "I don't want you to get hurt."

"Oh no, Nana, don't worry. It's just pretend," I explain. "And I'm very careful." Don't adults remember what it's like to pretend?

It's what happens to Wolf when he wears his army uniform. The teachers at school worry that Wolf is going to "injure someone someday with the way he behaves." They tell him right in the middle of class that "war hurts people," and that "he's too young to be a soldier." Wolf doesn't say a word; he just stares down into his notebook. The teachers sigh, shrug, and go right back to talking about fractions or whatever.

09:37

I search the street with my silver binoculars. I spot Wolf rounding the corner and sneaking along the dirt paths. He whistles the mourning dove signal as a greeting before jumping into the trench with me.

"Sergeant Salazar, did you find your dad?"

"Negative, Captain," I say.

He slumps over for a second, disappointed. "We'll keep searching," he reassures me. "But first, we've got to do extra preparations this morning," he commands.

I don't want to tell Wolf that my mom won't let me call my dad's phone number. I don't really want to explain that my mom thinks my dad doesn't care enough to see me. So I simply say, "Yes, sir, Captain McCann. Like what?"

"No less than twenty mud balls lined up and ready to go, ten water balloons, and four stinky bombs."

Stinky bombs are a new invention. I steal Johnny's dirty socks, the smelliest items known to humanity, and then fill them with dirt. Gloves are required because we can't risk contamination. We tie the socks at the end, whip them in circles over our heads until they are fast and unpredictable, and then, finally, release them.

"Yes, sir. This should be no problem," I assure him. "Diego's gone to his swimming lesson and is not expected to return 'til thirteen hundred hours."

"Not good enough, soldier." Since jumping into the trench, Wolf has not made eye contact with me. He is climbing from one end of the hole to the other, scanning all the way from the corner north of us to the bend in Muscatel south of us.

"New intel was obtained last night," Wolf says. "I was trying to steal a Snickers bar at Fred's Liquor. I was crouched down and I was quiet." Wolf takes a drink from his canteen and continues, speaking quickly and seriously. "At approximately nineteen hundred hours, Greg and Doug Wilson entered the store. They bought two Like Colas, one bag of Cheetos, and another bag of barbecue chips. They spoke about coming to the new Muscatel dirt track to try out their bikes today. To our street! They did not identify my location."

Even though Wolf doesn't actually live on my street, he spends so much time hanging out with me here that he's like an honorary member. So I don't mind that he thinks of it as his street, too. I actually kind of like it. It is, however, definitely not Greg and Doug's street.

"Oh no!" I say.

Greg and Doug are the worst kids at school. They live right at the top of the city and act like they're better than other people. Anyone who lives near the freeway, like us, is a lower life-form. They know mean words, and use them. I can't believe they would even bother to come down to our street.

10:18

We act fast and make almost all the required weapons by the time Greg and Doug round the corner on their bikes. They have big clunky bikes with thick tires. The brothers are jumping over the tiny bridges in the dirt that Johnny and his friends made out of wood and bricks. They are splashing through the little stream that the smallest Eftychiou brother from down the street makes with his garden hose when his mom is out shopping. Greg and Doug, who don't belong here, are laughing and enjoying our street.

It should be fine. We renovated the street for kids to play on. It's our own summer carnival, made by and for kids. But Greg and Doug are bigger than us, and if we have to

fight them, it will hurt. I think maybe, if we're quiet enough, they don't have to know we're here.

We lean against the side of the trench and don't make a single sound while they ride around above us. I close my eyes and wait and hope that they go away. The problem is that the air grows thin in the trench, and there's not enough for me to breathe. I put my hands on my chest and feel myself breathing faster and faster.

"Oh no," I whisper to Wolf. "We're running out of air."

"No, Alex," he pleads. "Trust me, there's plenty of air."

It doesn't feel like it. Why does my body always fall for this?

"Please, stop it. Please, just breathe." I try to convince myself. "I can't jump out of this trench, right now. Alex, listen! There's enough oxygen, just please breathe."

Right when I'm sure I won't be able to take it anymore, Doug almost slides into our trench while speeding around the figure-eight track. At first, he is scared. He gulps a bunch of air and his eyes spring wide open when his leg drops halfway into the trench. But then he stops moving. He takes a big breath and closes his eyes.

We don't know what to do. We could start firing bombs now, but even if it is Doug Wilson, it seems unfair to bomb a kid when he's crashed partly down a hole on his bike.

Doug opens his eyes, looks down, and sees us. His eyebrows are scrunched up in confusion, but then he recognizes our faces. He begins to smile, but it's not a nice smile. It's a crooked smile that means he's thinking of something bad to do.

"Hey, Greg," he yells. "Look at this!"

Greg peers down into our trench and shakes his head. "Look at all this nice equipment you've got for us: binoculars, sleeping bags, Snickers. I'll take that canteen." He laughs. "What do you want, Doug?"

"You're not taking anything," Wolf says defiantly. "Get off our street. We don't want you here."

Greg repeats Wolf's words in a high-pitched voice. "You're not taking anything."

Doug says, "Oh yeah? What do we have here, Greg? Two little gays in a hole."

"You're the gay," I shout back.

Doug laughs. "You don't even know what that word means, do you?"

"Yeah, I do," I say confidently. Except, I really don't. All the kids at school say it, but nobody ever really says what it means.

"Dude," Greg says, "that kid's not gay. That's a girl. I mean, I think it's a girl."

"Ewwww," Doug says. And then he stares at me, opening his mouth too wide. "What are you, anyway? A boy or a girl? You can't decide, or what?"

Greg crouches down even closer to me. "And are you a Mexican? Or are you white? Wasn't your dad a white guy? Where is he, anyway?"

Wolf steps in front of me to block Greg. "Leave her alone. I'm warning you."

Doug chuckles. "And you're the crazy Rambo Boy, aren't you? Is your family so poor they can't buy you real clothes?"

That's when we start firing. We whirl our stinky bombs around and smack them with water balloons. We throw mud balls, we punch, we shout.

They spit down on us. It's disgusting. They call us dirt. They kick mud into our hole.

But we've got a big stockpile of weapons, and we keep throwing. We throw as hard as we can. I'm so mad that every piece of mud that splatters on their bodies feels magnificent. Wolf gets something in Doug's eye. While he's trying to get it out, Greg is yelling at him to keep fighting, but he can't. He is bent over, trying to get the dirt out of his eye.

"Dude," Doug says, "I told you we shouldn't have come down here. They're not worth the dirt they live in."'

"Yeah, well, it's our dirt and not yours!" I say.

"Yeah, get off our dirt!" Wolf yells.

"You guys are losers," Greg says, stepping away from our trench. "Let's get out of here."

They pull their bikes out of the mud, jump on their pedals, and ride off our street.

Wolf and I cheer and hug each other, celebrating our victory.

"We did it! We did it! The street belongs to us!"

chapter 13

STREET PARTY

Monday afternoon. 13:17.

Diego walks slowly down the street with a little duffel bag thrown over his shoulder. Under the midday sun, all traces of his swim have evaporated. He is hot and sweaty as he turns the corner back onto Muscatel Avenue.

Captain McCann and I don't make a sound inside our trench. Wolf watches Diego closely through my binoculars. He lifts his arm, holds his fist out, and opens it slowly. It's the sign that someone is coming. I reach down into the cool muddy corner of the trench and gently pull up two pink water balloons. I offer one to the captain and cradle the other in my hands.

Diego's pace slows as he gets closer to home. Now he has to trudge through the soft, baked mud of our street. He takes his shoes off and starts squishing his way past our trench. Wolf signals by moving his whole arm down once, twice, and on the third time, we throw our balloons up in the air and at our target. Wolf's balloon breaks and splashes down all over both of us, but mine clears the trench and bursts against Diego's back.

Diego shrieks and we cheer, even though we're soaking wet, too. When Diego turns around, we brace ourselves for a counterassault. But instead of yelling at us or running away, he lunges toward us.

Wolf raises his hand straight up, then turns his wrist back and forth twice.

At the same time, I yell, "Let's get out of here!"

But Diego is faster than us and leaps into our trench before we can escape. Each of us scrapes mud off the walls, grabs mud balls, and tries to stomp on water balloons. We are having the biggest mud fight of all time. Diego's laughing, and so are we.

That's when we hear Jaime from across the mud road calling, "Diego? Diego, are you there?"

The three of us are giggling hard, but being in a big hole in the ground makes it difficult for anyone else to hear us.

"Diego?" Jaime asks, wandering toward our trench. "I thought I heard you."

Diego looks at us sternly with his finger over his lips. We are silent.

We can hear Jaime walking slowly toward our trench. "Diego?"

I am trying not to breathe. I look down and spot one last intact pink water balloon. I hand it carefully to Diego. He waits until Jaime is pretty much on top of us, and then flings it across his chest.

"Arggh!" Jaime yells. "You double-crosser!" And then he leaps in on top of the rest of us.

Once we're all good and muddy and tired and sitting together at the bottom of our trench, Wolf and I tell Jaime and Diego what happened with Greg and Doug Wilson.

"They said we live in dirt," I say, outraged, covered in dirt.

Wolf shakes his head and adds, "But we beat them and made them leave."

Diego and Jaime look at each other and nod.

"What?" Wolf says.

"This calls for a street party," Jaime says.

They head off in separate directions to knock on doors, telling everyone that there is going to be an official street party. I run inside the house quick and change my wet shirt for a dry one, so that my puffy right nipple doesn't show through the shirt for everyone to see.

We claim different parts of the street to set up activities. Jaime says we could run the party as our very own Olympics. The Muscatel Avenue 1984 Olympic Games. I smooth out a patch of dirt near the fire hydrant to make a marble-playing event; Wolf invents speed trench climbing; Diego makes a soccer-kicking challenge; Jaime runs the mud ball throw (with extra points for landing a mud ball clear across the wash and into someone's swimming pool), and the giant figure-eight bike track remains the most popular attraction. Realizing the financial possibilities of the newly formed mini-Olympics, Clarissa Brown from five doors down sets up a temporary tattoo table; the Vega family decides it's a good opportunity for a yard sale; Ronny Graham is giving the little kids rides on his bike; my nana reheats some beans and makes a tostada table; and Old Mrs Hoganson from two doors down slices up a watermelon.

When Tony gets home, he wants to set up a break-dancing competition. Wolf remembers the old fence in our garage and we drag it out to make a platform for the stage. This challenges Johnny to make his own entertainment area, which turns out to be a boom box blasting heavy metal. We

convince him that it would be cooler to play it down in the wash where it will echo and leave the rest of us somewhat free of all the screaming songs.

I am eating watermelon to cool off beside my marble-playing arena and helping the little kids with thumb shots. There are kids playing and running in every direction on our street, many of whom I don't even recognize. I move my chin up and down to Michael Jackson's "Beat It" while the break-dancing boys twist their sweaty bodies up diagonally and swirl to the music. They move like the tops you pull fast with a string. Wolf is over at the trench, eagerly explaining mud ball-making to the Wong sisters from the other side of the wash. My nana is on her little lawn chair, smiling and clapping along, watching all the kids at play along our dirt street. Even my mom has taken a seat beside my nana, her head deep in a thick, new paperback.

"Alex, this is a celebration of the land!" my nana yells out to me.

I don't want to confess to her about the way we beat those awful Wilson boys with mud balls and decided to celebrate, so I just nod. "Yes, Nana."

"The land wants to be adored," she explains. "And you kids know best how to do it." She grins at me.

A big smile spreads across my face. Those Wilson boys and their mean words hurt my feelings, but my nana always makes me feel better.

Monday evening. 20:38.

The street party is loud and full of the whole neighborhood, so I don't notice anything is wrong until I hear Wolf. I see Mr McCann's back as he leans over the trench, and I can hear Wolf screaming, "I didn't do anything wrong!" and "Dad, you're not listening!" and "It was the Wilson kids that were jerks!" and "No, I'm not going anywhere with you!"

My mom and I quickly move over to the action. She goes to Mr McCann, and I go to Wolf. He is sitting on the bottom of the trench, hugging his knees. I say his name a couple of times, but he won't answer and he won't look up.

My mom touches Mr McCann's arm and he turns to her. His face is red from the heat, but his eyes are big and confused.

"I got a call from Myrna Wilson an hour ago, saying they are considering pressing charges against Wolf." He takes a breath. "Seems Wolf punched and threw mud at her boys."

"But that's not what happened–" The words shoot out of my mouth before my mom cuts me off.

"Let him speak, mija."

"The thing is," he explains, "Wolf's already on the police's radar from the incident last year at school, when he threw his book across the assembly hall and it hit the principal in the nose." Mr McCann tosses his hands in the air. "I don't know how to control him."

"But they started it!" I manage to yell out. "The Wilson brothers picked a fight with us!" If I can tell them the truth, Wolf will stop being in trouble.

My mom turns to me. "Alex, even if it wasn't his fault, it could be bad for Wolf if the police get involved." She continues. "Sometimes they listen," she takes a breath, "and sometimes they don't."

"How do they decide which to do?" I ask nervously.

"Depends on the color of your skin. Depends on what neighborhood you come from. Depends on whether they think you're a good type of person or a bad one. Depends on whether they had a good day or a bad day."

Mr McCann nods.

By now about a dozen kids have gathered around us to lean over the trench and stare down at Wolf. They are asking questions: "What's going on?" and "Who is that?" and "Is that the crazy Rambo kid?" and "Did you hear what happened to Doug and Greg Wilson?"

I scream back at them, "He's not crazy! Stop saying that!"

My mom breaks in with a calm but forceful voice. "Can you all back up and give us some room, please?"

She asks Tony to put on a new song so that the dancing can start again. And she instructs me to jump down into the trench to try to coax Wolf out.

I climb into the trench and sit next to Wolf but not too close. "Those kids don't know anything," I say. "And Doug and Greg are liars."

Wolf won't look at me, but he does nod a little.

"If the cops come, I'll be with you," I assure him. "I'll tell them exactly how everything happened."

"Okay," he mumbles.

A police helicopter starts circling over our street, and Johnny screams at it from the wash, "Man, you're messing up my music. Go away!"

"I think we should get out of here," I tell Wolf.

"Yeah," he whispers.

Wolf gets up, brushes the mud off his pants, climbs out of the trench, and starts jogging down the street. By the time I pull myself out, he is already halfway to the corner, with his dad hurrying behind him.

chapter 14

THE BUD

Monday night. 21:46.

It's one of those nights that doesn't really cool off, and I'm not feeling too well. The street party is over. It never recovered after Wolf left. I don't know when I'll get to talk to him to see if he's okay. I don't know if the police will try to take him away. I lost my dad, and I don't want to lose anyone else. I don't know why Doug and Greg Wilson were talking about my dad.

My nana pours cold water over a washcloth and rolls an ice cube in the middle.

"Are you sick, Alex?" she asks.

"No, Nana. I'm hot from running around outside," I reassure her.

"When the Spanish flu came around my skin was very hot," she tells me. "I would lie down all day and watch the white sheet in the doorway, waving in the wind. I could hear the horse carriage coming down our street to collect the bodies." She shakes her head. "It's a miracle I survived."

"Really, Nana, I'm okay, just a little overheated," I try to explain.

She always tells the Spanish flu story whenever I'm even a little bit sick. It freaks me out every time, thinking I could die.

"You never know when the Spanish flu will hit again," she warns and hands me the washcloth. "Rub it on your forehead and the back of your neck."

It feels soothing at first, but then the washcloth slowly becomes as hot as my skin. I go into my mom's room and lie on the bed beside her with the fan blowing on us. She's on the phone with her best friend, Carol. They are gossiping about people, and my mom uses initials for names so that I won't repeat anything in front of the wrong person.

"M shouldn't have told X about what happened at the street party, but X was still being too sensitive," she says.

When she gets off the phone, she turns on her side and looks at me. "You worried about Wolf?"

"Do you think Dad is ever coming back?" I ask.

Her head jerks back. "I don't know." She strokes my hair. "He wasn't very good at being in a family." She sighs. "And he doesn't like doing things he's not good at."

I blink against the wet in my eyes. "I love him anyway."

"I know, mija." She squeezes my hand.

I nestle my head in her armpit. I feel her chest rise and fall.

I think about my own chest. My sore heart inside. I haven't been able to bring myself to open the bag with the medical book. I don't want to find out I'm gonna die. My mom will be so sad if have to leave her, too.

If I don't find out, then I can just lie here next to her cozy body. I squish into her and try to fall asleep.

My mom starts snoring.

I really love my mom, but her snoring is annoying.

I push her arm aside and sneak out of the room.

22:04

I find my backpack under the desk in my bedroom. I dig inside and pull out the deed to Aztlán. It's pretty, with the old-fashioned writing and the shiny gold seal. It makes sense now that it was made by an artist. I like that people dream about Aztlán and it makes them feel safe. I tack it up on my bulletin board.

I have to know what's wrong with my heart.

I pull the brown bag from my backpack and stick it on my desk. I close my eyes tight and slide the medical book out of the bag. I open my eyes a sliver and peek at the title: *THE NEW OUR BODIES, OURSELVES: A Book by and for Women.*

I close my eyes again, fast. What the heck? What the heck do women have to do with hearts? The librarian must've made a mistake. I don't want a book about women. Yuck!

I've gotta hide this and get it back to the library before anyone sees it.

When I turn the book around to stash it back in the bag, I feel a sticky note poking out of the side. Hmm.

I open the page to find the title "Breast Development." There is an arrow on the sticky note pointing to the line, "A firm mass develops directly behind the nipple. This is called the bud." Above the arrow, the librarian wrote, "Sometimes this can hurt."

Oh no! Terrible! Gross! I'm getting breasts like a woman? These things are going to grow big like my mom's? Like the women on Johnny's posters? How am I gonna find T-shirts big enough to hide them?

But I'm not a woman. I'm not going to be a woman. I don't think. I don't know. Maybe I am. At least I'm not going to die, but jeez.

"Hey, Alex," Johnny says as he bursts into my room.

I shut the book fast and throw a paper on top of it. I turn around quickly, with the book behind my back. "What do you want?"

"Nothing," he says.

"Really?"

"Really." He's got something dirty in his hand. He's walking around my room, looking at my stuff.

It's super weird because he hardly ever comes into my room.

"You know," he says, "you're usually only an irritation in my life."

"Wow, thanks," I say sarcastically.

"But I have to admit, I enjoyed that street party," he tells me. "Hearing Ozzy echo up and down the wash was awesome."

"Oh, I'm glad you liked it," I say awkwardly. "Maybe we can do another one next week?"

"No," he says. "That was good. But it was enough. I've gotta rehearse."

"Right," I say.

He is looking around at my photos and drawings when his eyes stop above my desk. "Oh wow," he says. "Where'd you find that?"

I follow his eyes to the deed of Aztlán. "Buried in a bag next to the rosebush," I say. "It was really weird."

"Hm." He nods. "That makes sense. He put it in with his roses."

I stand up, a bit shocked. "What do you mean?"

"That belongs to Dad. That's what he blew all his money on, the night Mom kicked him out."

"What are you talking about?!"

"Yeah, I guess you were already asleep when he came home." Johnny stands close to the paper, tracing his fingers over the embossed letters of the deed. "You know how Nana always talks about how important Aztlán is. He thought it was real. He thought he bought us Aztlán."

"That's so sweet," I say, my eyes getting wet.

"Mom didn't think so," Johnny says bitterly. "She was ticked that he lost a bunch of our money, so she kicked him out."

"But I thought he left us," I say.

"Oh, sure." He shakes his head. "She only says that so that it's not her fault."

"That's terrible!" I cry out.

"It's whatever." Johnny shrugs and starts toward the door but then stops. "Oh yeah, there's one more thing," he says.

"What is it?" Maybe he knows something more about our dad.

He opens his hand up and reveals a muddy sock. "I found this in the wash," he says, kind of puzzled. "I think it's one of my socks."

"Whoa," I say, feeling sick to my stomach. I'm sure he's going to figure out I turned his socks into muddy stink bombs.

"It must've gotten sucked up into the washing machine and squirted out into the wash," he explains. "Isn't that a trip?"

"Totally," I say, relieved.

He turns back around and leaves me alone in my bedroom once more.

I fall down onto the floor and sit there, crying, hugging my legs. I scrunch my hair in my hands over and over and think. So he wasn't mad at me. But why would my mom kick Dad out? He was only trying to do something nice for us. He didn't know Aztlán wasn't real. In my nana's stories everything sounds real. It's not fair!

I go sit on my bed and cry and hold Hops the Kangaroo tight.

22:31

The phone rings and jolts me out of my tears. I scramble as fast as I can to my mom's room to pick up the phone. Her eyes blink open.

I hear Wolf's voice. "First, don't say anything to alert your mom that there's a problem. Do you understand?"

"Yeah, sure," I say casually.

My mom is looking at me with half-open eyes. I turn away so that she can't see my own red and swollen eyes.

"It's Wolf," I tell her. "It's fine."

It's not fine and I'm mad at her, but I don't want her to get up.

"Meet me in the trench at twenty-three thirty," Wolf says. "Bring any provisions available. Also, grab as many Ziplocs as you can."

"I'm glad you're feeling better," I say, trying to sound like he's not being a big weirdo. I don't know why he has to have a plan for everything instead of just telling me what's going on.

We hang up and I tell my mom that Wolf wanted to let me know he was okay.

23:04

There is finally silence in the house. I creep around in my socks and find my way by the lavender light in the hallway that helps the plants grow. I open the cupboard beneath the sink and grab the whole box of plastic Ziploc bags. My mom's going to kill me for this. She hates when we waste them, but I don't care what she says anymore.

Very slowly, I crack open the fridge door. Wolf's in luck. There's a big hunk of turkey pastrami for sandwiches. I slip it into my duffel bag and grab a half-full container of margarine. I crack open the freezer door and pull out a bag with five and a half frozen bagels. This should do it. Even if Wolf's pulling an all-night plan, he can't eat this much. I fill my canteen with water and throw it in the bag, too.

I exit through the back door because it's quieter. I toss my stuff into the trench, and then lower myself down beside it. I look up at the sky and wait. The city lights blur all but a couple of stars. Even if it is muddy in the trench, it still feels better down here in the dirt. I'm glad I'm out of the house and away from my mom. Maybe this is how my dad feels. Why did she have to be so mean to him?

23:47

Ugh. Wolf's late. I'm going to kill him. He's my best friend, but I'm going to kill him. When is he going to get here–

I hear the mourning dove call and Wolf jumps down into the trench. He's wearing his full fatigues and cap. He's got a duffel bag over his shoulder that looks too heavy for him to carry. A drip of sweat trickles down his face.

"It's too hot for all those clothes," I complain, tired and frustrated.

He ignores me. "Sergeant Salazar?"

"Yes, Captain McCann," I say, yawning.

"I will be departing at zero zero fifteen hours," he states, and turns away from me.

I jump up. "Departing where?"

"Across Los Angeles and out to the ocean," Wolf says, his voice emotionless. "Look." He pulls out a flashlight and a map and traces the wash south with his finger, through Pico Rivera, Downey, Lakewood, Long Beach.

"What are you talking about?" I ask.

"It's time for me to go," he explains.

"The cops tried to get you?!" I gasp. "Why didn't you call? I would've come to help."

"No, they haven't come yet," he admits, as he starts zipping and unzipping pockets on his jacket and pants and stuffing supplies from the trench into them.

"Then there's no reason to go anywhere," I argue.

"There's something else," he whispers, and looks at me.

I'm scared. "What is it?"

He gulps. "My dad and his girlfriend are getting married."

"So?!" I exclaim.

"So, they're happy together. But I'm not. I'm not part of it." He lifts his cap and wipes his eyes. "I don't want to be part of it, and I cause a lot of trouble, so it's better if I leave."

"It's not better, Wolf." I'm getting mad.

I flip on my flashlight and catch sight of a tear coming out of his eye. He pushes the flashlight down fast. "I'm not crying," he says.

"I know," I say, because that's what he wants me to say. I try to reason with him. "You can't carry this stuff all the way to the ocean."

"I've already planned this out. I'm going to rig my duffel bag to the old fence–to my raft–and pull it down the middle of the wash," Wolf explains.

"The sheriffs are always circling the city, Wolf. They'd like nothing better than to catch you and drive over to your home and make a whole big deal out of it. And then your dad would threaten to take your army uniform away again, or worse." I say, desperate. "And it would be a big mess, okay? A big mess!"

"No, they won't," he answers angrily. "They won't catch me. They won't find me in the wash. By morning, I'll be halfway to the Pacific."

Wolf can't go like this. He can't leave and never come back. He can't do that. He'll get hurt out there where nobody knows him.

"Why do you want to go to the ocean anyway?" The longer I keep him talking, the longer he is with me and not gone.

Wolf wipes his tears away and takes a quick breath. "Whenever my mom got too upset, she would pack a picnic and drive me and my dad to the ocean with her," he explains. "That's where you go when you're too upset."

I'm picking at the mud on the side of the trench wall. I rub my hands in it. I try to think of the words that will keep my friend from leaving.

"Wolf, you can't find your mom at the ocean," I tell him. "She wouldn't want you to be there all by yourself." I smell the mud on my fingers and look up at the dark sky. "Besides, we could get our parents to drive us there on a Saturday."

I take a deep breath. "Actually," I say, "I think the closest you can ever be to your mom is right here inside our trench, inside the dirt," I swallow. "I mean, it's where we come from. And it's where we go after we die."

"I'm not dead, Alex." Wolf's voice grows cold. "I just need a different place to live."

"I didn't mean that. Ugh." I get so frustrated. Wolf makes his plans and doesn't listen. I throw a rock up and out of the trench.

Wolf stands up and brushes the dirt from his pants. "Sergeant Salazar, I have to head out now."

I won't take this as an answer. I try again with my words. "The dirt makes all the plants grow. The dirt is where we've been safe all summer. The dirt is where everyone leaves us alone. We can stay here together, Wolf. The dirt is ours."

And even though these are the best words I've ever come up with, Wolf is still climbing up the ladder.

"Wait!" I shout. "Then I'm coming with you."

chapter 15

SET SAIL

Tuesday morning. 00:07.

"You can't come with me," Wolf argues. "What about your mom?"

"My mom betrayed me," I say.

His eyes get big. "What do you mean? What happened?"

"I found out where the deed came from." I fill Wolf in on how my mom tried to deny that it was my dad's phone number. Then stopped me from calling him. Then told me he didn't want to see us. Then how Johnny knew the deed was my dad's, how my dad wanted to give us Aztlán, but it wasn't actually real, and then my mom got mad at him for losing our money, and then she threw him out.

"Wow," he says, shaking his head. "That's awful."

"Take me with you as far as Downey. Then I'll climb out and find my dad, and you can go on your way." I hold my hand out to him. "Agreed?"

He thinks about it for a moment, and then reaches out to shake my hand. "Agreed, Sergeant Salazar. Do you need to get anything from the house?"

"Nope." I've been carrying the little paper with my dad's information on it in my pocket ever since the day in the kitchen with my mom. That's all I need. "Let's go."

We hoist Wolf's stuff over the chain-link fence and let it drop down into the wash. The raft is the hardest part, so we lift it together, balance it on top of the fence, and wait for Wolf to scramble over and grab it again on the other side. Once we have all the stuff down inside the wash, Wolf begins to secure the supplies to the raft with ropes and bungee cords.

He takes the Ziploc bags I gave him and puts inside a photo of his mom and dad, his wallet, his school ID card, and his camera. He double-bags them to keep them from getting wet or messed up.

He ties one of the ropes from the raft around his waist and throws me the other. I secure it around me, and we give the raft a push into the little algae stream. It begins to move

slowly with the current, and we walk ahead of it, on either side of the water, pulling it along.

Wolf looks over at me and smiles. "I'm glad you're coming with me."

Tuesday morning. 01:07.

"One beat that's a short low tone, then a long one that goes up and down, and then another couple low tones. Like this." Wolf whistles.

He is teaching me how to make a mourning dove call. It sounds really cool and loud down in the wash in the middle of the night. We whistle it together, but mine sounds fake. I think my mouth's not big enough for all the notes.

When there's a rock in the wash, each of us gives it a good hard kick, and then we watch it skip and dance thirty feet ahead of us, bouncing off the concrete walls. A couple of times we've even managed to make a rock hop the stream to the other side, so we can pass it back and forth between us.

We come upon a tree branch with a big clump attached to it.

I turn away, because what if it's a dead rat or something?

"Hold up," Wolf says, and reaches down for the clump. It turns out to be a handful of algae.

"Ewww, gross. It's all slimy."

Wolf smiles up at me, his hands full of green gunk.

"I'm not touching you ever again." I back up.

He laughs and hurtles it at the wall. It splats a bunch of mud and falls down.

"Yessss!" he cries.

I look at the muddy wall and think of the notebook he threw–splat–at the principal's face during the assembly in March. Nobody yelled, nobody cheered, nobody made a sound, besides the principal's loud, "Owwww! Crap!" Which was kind of like swearing, but none of the kids gave him a hard time on account of the blood that started pouring out of his nose. The principal had been in charge of a room of two hundred kids, and then a second later, he was bent over, dripping bright red blood.

The gym teacher jumped up and yanked Wolf out of the auditorium. That prank got him kicked out of school for, like, the hundredth time, but they called the police for this one, and they didn't let him come back to finish the year. That's why Wolf spends his days at the library.

"Hey, Wolf," I ask. "Why did you throw the notebook at the principal anyway?"

"You heard him," he says. "He accused me of talking in the back."

"Yeah, I know, but he always goes around the room, asking kids to be quiet."

"But I wasn't talking," Wolf says defensively.

"I mean," I look at Wolf and say tentatively, "you were actually talking. I was sitting right next to you."

"Okay, yeah, but a lot of kids were talking, and I wasn't talking any louder than them."

"Well, that's true," I concede.

"He yelled out, 'Wolf, keep quiet!' in front of all those kids," he says. "And I could hear them start laughing." He kicks at another rock, which smacks against the wall and rolls back over into the stream.

He looks away from me so I can't see his face. "I was so sick of hearing kids laugh at me. I was so sick of going to school and pretending like everything was normal and my mom wasn't dead." Wolf pauses. "And I didn't want to keep quiet anymore."

I feel so bad for him. I want to go to him and pat his back or something. I start crossing the little algae stream, but when the rope from the raft tugs at me, I slip and fall.

"Oh, yuck!" I shout.

I'm lying flat on my stomach in the slime with water streaming through my pants and shirt. I roll over, sit up, and look at my drenched body.

Wolf starts giggling. "*I'm* never gonna touch *you* again."

I'm fully grossed out, but his giggling starts up my giggling. He unloops the rope from his belt and does his Dodgers slide into the stream next to me, splashing any part of me that wasn't already wet.

"Argh!" I yell, turning my head away from the spray.

He jumps on me and we start wrestling, rolling on the concrete together. He pins me down, and then I push with all my strength and knock him off me.

I lie on top of him. "I'm stronger than you, Wolf."

"Yeah, yeah, I know," he says. "But only if you keep your training up." He nudges me, and I move off him.

We sit in the water together, looking at each other and laughing. My body is finally cooling down in the early-morning desert air.

"You could've just told me you wanted to stop for a swim," Wolf jokes.

"Shut up."

"You should've seen yourself. Full-fledged belly flop." He giggles some more.

I laugh with him for a bit. Then I look down and see my left nipple poking up a little and my right nipple puffing way out under my wet shirt.

"Oh no!" I exclaim, and cover my chest quickly with my arms.

Wolf pulls back, startled. "What's wrong?"

My face goes red. "Nothing."

"No, something's wrong," he says.

"It's embarrassing," I answer.

"More embarrassing than your belly flop?" he asks incredulously.

"Yeah," I answer with certainty.

"Wow," he says. "Tell me anyway."

"No way."

"Look, you should tell me," he insists.

"Why?"

"Let's see," he says, holding up his fingers to count. "Number one, I'm your best friend. Number two, I just told you why I threw the book at the principal. Number three, it's dark, and it's easier to tell things in the dark."

"Okay," I say. "But don't laugh."

"Not a chance."

I lower my arms and look down at my swollen chest.

"What?"

"Look at them," I say.

"Look at what?"

"Oh, come on, can't you see how big my chest has gotten?"

"Oh, huh. I hadn't noticed," he says, staring more closely at me. "I can see that one." He points at the right nipple.

"Jeez, don't point."

"Oh, sorry," he says, lowering his finger. "Hey, how come one's bigger than the other?"

"I don't know!"

"I didn't mean to make you mad," he says. "I was just curious."

"I know. It's okay," I say. "I wish I knew more about what's happening to me."

"Well, it's probably fine," he says. "They probably just grow when they're ready. I was reading about orangutan development during lactation and they say that–"

"I'm not an orangutan, Wolf."

"Yeah, I know, but they're primates like us, and there might be some facts that are helpful." He stops talking when he sees I have my hands over my face.

"Wolf, I don't know *what* I am. If I'm a girl or a boy? If I'll be a woman or, or, a man or what!"

"So?"

"Well, these are coming." I point to my chest. "And then I won't be able to hide them, and I'll have to be a woman."

"That doesn't make sense," he says. "We're animals. Some animals are boys or girls and some aren't. And some change. It's not such a big deal. Like seahorses, when they want to have babies–"

"Wolf, it might not be a big deal to animals, but it's a big deal to people."

"Oh, yeah, you could be right." He nods.

"What am I going to do?" I ask.

"Hmm, I'm not very good with people, so I don't know what to say about them." He pauses to consider the situation. "But I don't think a chest growing big automatically makes you a woman. It must be up to you. If you decide to be a guy, then your chest, whatever it looks like, will be a guy's chest because it's yours. And if you decide to be a woman, well, then logically, it's the opposite."

"Really?"

"Yeah, I think so," he says. "Scientifically, it would be impossible for someone outside of your body to know what your body feels like inside. You're the only one that would have access to that data. I could find a library in Long Beach and try to get some more material on it, though."

"Oh yeah? I'd really like that," I say, standing up and brushing bits of leaves and dirt off my pants.

He stands up beside me and walks over to grab his rope. He ties it around himself and we continue on our trek.

Tuesday morning. 04:36.

My legs are dying when Wolf suddenly stops and studies the bridge above us. "This is it." Wolf points. "Florence Avenue."

"We made it?"

"Yep. You climb up this ladder," he says as he studies the map, "then head east on Florence, south on Paramount, east again on Third, and then south on Myrtle. It's really only a mile or two more."

"So I'm going left and then right? And then left and right again?"

"Not exactly."

"Hmm."

"Shoot, I'd give you my map, but I kind of need it."

"That's okay," I say. "I'm sure I'll be able to find it." I lower my head. "Wolf, you're my best friend. You better be careful. And you better write to me so that I know where you live and that you're okay."

"I'll send you a postcard as soon as I make it to the beach," he promises.

"I still don't want you to go," I say. "I still think it's a bad idea."

"I know, but I still gotta go," he says.

He is standing with the rope tied around his waist and his raft beside him, smiling and ready for his adventure. There is nothing more to be said. He salutes me, and I salute him back and turn before any tears can fall out of my eyes. I climb up the ladder, hop over the fence, and head on my way.

chapter 16

WHAT ABOUT ME?

The street is dark and empty. It gives me the creeps, so I try to walk fast. There are tall fences and warehouses and telephone poles but mostly nothing. I start breathing faster and faster, and my fingers begin to twitch.

"No, Alex," I tell myself. "No panic attack out here when you're all alone." I hear myself and breathe even faster. "Oh jeez, I'm scared." I begin to jog.

All of a sudden, a finger taps my shoulder and I scream, "Argggh! Don't touch me!"

"Alex, don't freak out. It's just me," Wolf says.

"You scared the heck out of me!" I say, panting.

"Sorry about that," he says. "It's just that I waited to watch what direction you would walk, and as I suspected, you went the wrong way."

"Oh." I feel kind of dumb now.

"Look," he says. "I tied my raft to the ladder. It should be safe for a while. I've got the map. I'll walk with you to your dad's house. It shouldn't take too long."

"I'm not sure," I say.

I'm not sure if I want him with me when I find my dad. I've been dreaming too long about finding him and hugging him and telling him how much I love him, and I don't think I can really do that in front of Wolf.

I think Wolf understands because he says, "I could just go with you as far as his house, and then leave when he opens the door?"

"Yeah, I guess that would be okay," I say. "I would like to actually find him."

And I am glad to have more time with Wolf.

Tuesday morning. 05:15.

It's a small peach-colored house with white trim. The yard is full of cacti, and there's a beautiful line of roses beside the house. For sure it belongs to my dad.

I breathe in and out slowly. I fill up my lungs and release all the air until they feel completely empty. Wolf is on the other side of the street, watching. I look over at him and he motions for me to knock on the door. I look down. I try breathing again. I can just stand here and practice breathing, I decide. I'm not the best at it. A little more practice wouldn't hurt.

Wolf runs up next to me. "What are you doing?"

"Practicing breathing," I say.

"You're not going to stop breathing," he says. "It's actually impossible to physically stop breathing without something blocking your air."

"So?" I say, touching the stucco with my fingers. "Doesn't hurt to practice."

A little dog inside the house bursts into barking, and Wolf and I freeze, staring at each other. The door opens, and Wolf and I see a tall, hunched man looking down at us through the screen. At this point it would be too weird for Wolf to run away, so he stays put next to me.

"Hey, what are you two boys doing on my porch this early in the morning!" says the irritated man.

He looks beyond us out to the street, probably wondering how we got here. The man has silver hair, but I can see in his gray-blue eyes and small, soft chin that he is my dad. The little dog is still yapping away at us.

"You're Charles Richardson," I say, more stating a fact than asking a question.

"That's correct, son," my dad says.

"It's me," I say. "Alex."

"Oh, wow," he says. "Alex, you've grown so big. I'm sorry I didn't recognize you, honey." He looks me up and down. He glances over at Wolf in his army uniform and squeezes his eyebrows together, confused.

"This is my friend Wolf," I say.

"I better get going anyhow," Wolf says.

"Nonsense," my dad says. "There's nowhere to go at this hour." He opens the door wide. "Come. Come in."

Wolf and I walk into the living room. The place smells like the little white dog that is jumping on my legs. I pet him, and he licks my fingers and follows me in. There's a couch and a coffee table on one side and a recliner chair across from a big wooden console TV on the other. There's a bookshelf and a big framed photograph of a train.

"Have a seat," my dad says. "You must be chilly in those T-shirts. I'll make us some coffee."

I want to tell him that I don't drink coffee because I'm just a kid, but he's my dad and he's making something for me. I sit, quiet and amazed.

A plump woman with long dark hair and wearing a robe peeks out from the hallway. "It's so early, Charlie. What's going on?" she says.

"It's nothing, sweetheart," he says. "Go back to bed."

Nothing? I'm visiting him for the first time in three years and he says it's nothing? Who is she?

"Who is that?" I ask when he returns with three coffees.

"Oh, that's Lydia," he says. "She's kind of my girlfriend right now."

"Oh."

"So, what brings you here?" he asks.

"Ummm," I say. "I mean, you. I came to see you."

"Oh, that's real nice of you to visit your old dad." He smiles and takes a sip of his coffee.

"Well, yeah," I say. "I missed you."

"That's very thoughtful of you to come, Alex."

"Yeah," I say. "Um, did you miss me?"

"Yeah," he answers. "Sure I missed you." He looks around the room. "Hey, Alex, do you want an Amtrak baseball cap?" He brings it over to me. "That's where I work. Reservations and tickets. All day long I help people get from one place to another."

I want to tell him that I already know he works for Amtrak, that he worked there the whole time I was growing up with him. But I just say, "Oh," and accept the hat into my lap.

"We've had loads of new station renovations, and the Cardinal and the Carolinian are very popular out east, but the bulk of my business is with the Metroliner between San Diego and Los Angeles. People have been very happy about that one. Fewer stops," he notes.

"That's pretty neat, Mr Richardson," Wolf says.

"Dad," I say, "are you ever going to come home?"

He looks around the room, and then points to the photograph of the train. "That's a picture I took of the

Coast Starlight, just north of Santa Barbara," he says proudly. "It was stopped near the highway because one of the engines had shut off."

"Oh," I say. It is actually a beautiful picture, the silver train gleaming in front of the ocean. "I know it wasn't your fault, Dad. I know you thought the deed was real, and you were trying to buy a nice place for us to live."

"Don't worry yourself about that, honey. I shouldn't have been out gambling so late. I had a bit to drink, you know. That wasn't the best time for making big decisions." He sips his coffee.

"I forgive you, Dad," I say. "It's okay. I'm not mad at you over it."

He shakes his head. "I didn't really belong with your mother anymore. She was getting all that education. That's not so much my thing."

"But what about me? What about Johnny?" I ask.

"Oh, how *is* Johnny?"

"He's good," I say. "I think." I continue. "He plays music."

"That's nice," he says. "And your grandmother? She was always very sweet to me." He grins.

"She's good. She forgets a lot, though."

"Oh, that's too bad," he says.

"She's okay, mostly," I add. "But what about me, Dad? I've grown up a lot and I'm not so messy. And I eat everything on my plate."

"You've got a wonderful mother, Alex. So smart," he says. "I knew she'd be able to take good care of you and you'd grow up into a fine young lady."

"You're still my dad, though."

"You're right, honey," he says. "And you know what? Let me give you two a ride home."

"But–" I try to stop him.

"There's no easy way back on the RTD buses, especially not at this hour. And if we wait any longer, the traffic will be bad."

He gets up and grabs his keys from a little hook by the door. I put my full coffee down on the tray and Wolf copies me. We stand up and follow my dad.

"Wanna come for the ride, Spotty?" he asks the dog, who prances happily in a circle beside him.

"Uh, Dad," I say. "Wolf's not coming back to my house–"

"Before I pick up my stuff by the wash," Wolf finishes the sentence. "Would it be okay if we stopped for a moment at the corner of Florence and the LA River, Mr Richardson?"

I look at Wolf, confused. He only gives me a shrug.

"Certainly, son," my dad says. "That's next to the 710, right on our way."

A few minutes later, my dad and I are waiting in his car while Wolf hops back into the wash and out again with his big bag. My dad doesn't ask why Wolf is grabbing stuff from the wash, and I don't volunteer anything.

After twenty minutes of driving in complete silence, he pulls slowly into the wobbly dirt road that used to be Muscatel Avenue.

"What's all this construction?" he asks.

"The city's putting in sidewalks," I say.

"That'll be real nice for the community." He seems genuinely appreciative.

We all get out of the car, and my dad asks Wolf to take a photograph of us.

My dad and I stand in front of the car. He puts his arm around me stiffly. Spotty sticks his head out the window. Wolf snaps the shot.

"It was real great to see you, honey," Charles Richardson announces, before he climbs back into his Plymouth Reliant and drives away.

chapter 17

DOWN THERE IN THE DIRT TOGETHER

Tuesday morning. 06:49.

Wolf and I stand in my front yard. The grass is cool and wet, but the rising sun will soon burn off the dew.

"What the heck was that?" I say, crumpling the Amtrak hat in my hands.

Wolf shakes his head. "I don't know."

"My mom said he didn't want to see me," I admit. "But I didn't believe it."

My nose quickly fills with mucus that I try to sniff up. I push a tear off my cheek, bend down, and grab a big chunk of dirt from one of the piles. I crush it in my hand until all that's left is a smooth stone that was hiding in the middle. I throw it hard and fast over the fence and into the wash, listening to it click-clack against the concrete.

"Your mom is usually right," Wolf observes.

"She *is* usually right," I agree. "And she loves me a whole lot."

I stare at him. "What are you doing here, Wolf? Why didn't you keep going down to Long Beach?"

"Hold on a second and I'll explain." He walks over to our trench and throws his bag inside. He grabs hold of the ladder and motions for me to follow. I climb down and lie next to him on the bottom.

"Are you gonna tell me?" I ask again.

"Well." He clears his throat. "All this time, I've been thinking that my dad was a real jerk and didn't like me anymore."

"I know."

"No offense, Alex, but meeting your dad made me see the whole situation differently," he says.

"Yeah," I say. "Your dad does seem to care about you a lot, even if he gets mad at you sometimes."

"That's what I'm thinking," he says.

"So you're not going to leave me?"

"No, Alex," Wolf assures me. "I'm back for good now."

He puts his hand around mine, not to wrestle, or punch, or high-five each other, but just to hold it.

We don't talk anymore after that. My head is spinning with images of my dad, and his train photo, and his sort-of girlfriend, and Spotty the dog. I'm completely exhausted and Wolf's hand on mine calms me down. When I feel his body begin to twitch with sleep, my own begins to follow. We sleep soundly, down there in the dirt, together.

THE MORNING SUN

Tuesday morning. 07:19.

The phone starts ringing before anyone wakes up. Alex's mother answers and hears the hysterical voice of Wolf's father. Wolf is missing. Did he spend the night at Alex's house? One trip across the living room and into Alex's bedroom reveals a second missing child.

The grown-ups are very upset and on full alert. Johnny is annoyed when his mother wakes him up to ask if he knows where Alex has gone. He rolls his eyes and goes back to bed. He covers his head with a pillow as the police siren comes closer and closer to his house. Alex's nana cannot remember where Alex was last and is not quite sure who Wolf is until they show her a picture. She smiles and says, "El lobito." She falls back asleep and misses the rest of the early-morning drama.

Alex's mother serves coffee to Wolf's father, Wolf's father's fiancée, and the police. It is 7:30 a.m., then 8:30 a.m. The police ask the parents to come down to the station to fill out official reports.

It is ten a.m. when Nana makes her coffee, soft-boils an egg, and chews her toast. She sits down in front of the TV to watch another history special. But she can't hear the show very well because of the helicopter circling above the neighborhood. She raises her fist, shakes it, and shouts, "Fuera helicóptero!" But the pilot can't hear her. The children cannot hear her either, because when you lie at the bottom of a deep trench, the earth swallows up sound.

Nana can't see the picture on the TV very well because there is too much light coming in through the living room window. She begins to curse the morning sun, but then she remembers the sun rises on the other side of the house. Why, then, is the room filled with golden streams of light? She curses her memory for playing tricks on her and looks out the window to check.

Spilling out of Alex and Wolf's trench in the front yard are yellow, orange, pink, and red rays of luminescence, sparkling and twisting together up into the air.

Nana shakes her head and whispers to herself, "So that's where they are."

The only materials on earth valuable enough to cause a bright light to shine out of the ground are jewels, and children. She knows this because when she was a child in México she would follow the glow to help her abuelo find their family's buried jewelry. Nana knows that Alex would never wear any jewelry, which means that only a child could be hiding in the trench. And if she remembers correctly, there are two children missing.

Nana dips her toast into her egg yolk, certain that having a good breakfast first is the only way she can face the crowd that will show up when she shares the news.

Tuesday morning. 11:00.

"Oh, thank heavens! There they are!"

My mom's voice startles us awake, and I look up to see three concerned faces gazing down at us. Wolf and I climb out of the trench, very groggy.

My nana doesn't look surprised.

"You scared me half to death, Wolf!" Mr McCann shouts.

"Sorry, Dad," Wolf mutters.

Even though our parents are furious at us, they give us big hugs.

"There aren't many more days left before the street will be finished," I explain.

"And we really wanted to camp out down here," Wolf adds.

"But we didn't think you'd let us," I finish.

"I'm so sorry, Dad," Wolf says. "I love you."

Wolf's dad's eyes widen, and he takes a step back. "I love you too, son."

I squeeze my mom. "I love you so much, Mom."

"I love you too, mija," she says, holding me tight.

The police officer standing in the driveway glares at Wolf and warns us both to "Stay out of trouble, kids. Make sure to always let your parents know where you are."

"Yes, sir," Wolf answers.

He asks my mom to sign off on the report and pulls away in his cruiser.

We all head inside and my nana makes us some chorizo-and-egg burritos. For the next hour my mom and Wolf's dad go back and forth between telling us not to ever do something like this again, and telling us that they love us. Back and forth. Back and forth. Mad at us, and then happy we've returned. Crossing their arms and giving lectures. Petting our hair like we're puppies.

I'm so happy that I'm home. I'm so happy that I have my mom.

After lunch, my nana returns to the living room to watch PBS, Mom searches all over the kitchen for the Ziploc bags to pack up the leftovers, and Wolf's dad holds his son tightly to him.

"I couldn't have a family without you," he tells Wolf.

Wolf mumbles, "I know" into his dad's chest.

Before they leave, Wolf reminds me to restock the trench for our next battle.

"Just a pretend battle, right?" his dad warns him.

"Just pretend," Wolf agrees. "I promise."

Tuesday night. 22:20.

I lie in bed, giving a dirty look to Hops the Kangaroo, who is lying on the opposite side of the mattress.

"Why did he give you to me," I ask, "if he doesn't even care about me?"

Hops obviously doesn't answer. Maybe he doesn't know the answer. Maybe he wouldn't tell me even if he did. He just looks back at me with big dark eyes.

"What?" I say.

His eyes are shiny and tender.

"I'm giving you that whole side of the bed!"

Still no answer.

Darn, it's hard to stay mad at him. "Okay, come here then." I wrap my arm around him and tuck him under the blanket with me. "It's not your fault," I reassure him.

I think about my dad in his peach house with his rose-bushes. I don't understand why he doesn't want to see me. Maybe I'll figure it out someday, but not right now.

Right now, I'd rather think about Wolf walking beside me in the wash, with his raft drifting between us. His brown curls are bunched up at the rim of his cap. He is smiling, kicking at stones, as we travel together beneath the city lights. I hope his new appreciation for his dad will be enough to keep him around, but I can't be sure.

Right now, I just want to sleep in my clean, dry bed for a long time. The streetlight through the window catches the gold seal on the deed to Aztlán, making it sparkle. My nana's right about something. I do feel safe with my mom, and my nana, and even Johnny, in this house, on this street, in Aztlán. I belong to this place. This is my home.

When I wake up tomorrow morning, I'll call Wolf to come over. It'll be one of the last few days on our dirt street, before the machines return with their concrete to cover up the land once more.

acknowledgments

I would like to thank the several parent-and-children teams who read drafts and offered valuable feedback: Julie Cosgrove, Kieran Cosgrove, May Chazan, Zoey Hodson, Alex Hodson, Kelly McGuire, Aliya Salama, Noah Salama, Jen Goldberg, and Jacinto Goldberg Flores. I would also like to thank Katerina Cook, Hilary Cook, Elena Pendleton, Isabel Millán, Hershel Russell, and Susan Dion for their loving encouragement and careful reading of drafts. Thank you to my friends and colleagues for listening to my tomboy/butch/trans stories and for our conversations about writing, craft, and art: Cynthia Budgell, Miriam Davidson, Kelly Young, Christopher Rooney, Natalie Gillis, Lindsay Bereza, Ben Loucks, Abigail Wilson, Rachelle Bergen, Derek Newman-Stille, Tara Goldstein, Kate Reid, Juanita Spears, Sylvie Bérard, Cathy Bruce, Karen Shenfeld, and Sally Chivers; the many students in my teacher stories class; Lengua Latina crew Cecilia Vizcaíno, Brenda Zavala-Antunez, Adriana Alarcón, janet romero-leiva, Valeska Gomez-Castillo, Brenda Polar; and buddies Rusty Barceló, Rita Urquijo-Ruiz,

Linda Heidenreich, Yvette Saavedra, Anita Tijerina Revilla, Justine Hernandez, Aureliano DeSoto, Adriana Ayala, Julieta Fajardo, Annette Cavender, Barbara Brush, Caitlin Mori, Joëlle Reid, Liz Vlietstra, Paola Bohorquez, Dunja Baus, Julie Wong Barker, Deborah Berrill, Carol Mahoney, Denise Handlarski, Lisa Ortiz and Maggie Anderson.

In addition, thanks to Farzana Doctor, whose pandemic writing sprints helped get me across to the finish line. Thanks to Lisa Walter, who talked me through the complicated family relationships of this book. Thanks to Barb Taylor Coyle, my friend, film director, and fabulous motivator of artistic creation, who saved me with plot ideas in the midst of my writer's block.

Thanks to my family for their love: Elaine Jiménez McCann, Richard Pendleton, Brian Pendleton, David Pendleton, Rhoda Pendleton, Arlene Pendleton, Matt Pendleton, Shane Pendleton, Melissa Pendleton, Judith Caulfield, Carter Cook, Heather Cook, Chris Cargill, Lil Trillo, Dinah Cook, Jesse Cook, Nancy Cardwell, Luc Cook, Charlotte Cook, Garry Pejski, Tammy Sturge, and Celia Arden.

My kid said nobody would read a book without good images these days, so I am very thankful to Gabriela Godoy for her beautiful and expressive drawings and to

Jazmin Welch for lovely design on the page. Thanks to Trent University and the School of Education and the Department of Gender and Social Justice for supporting me and my writing in all its forms. Thanks to the writers of El Plan Espiritual de Aztlán, adopted by the First National Chicano Liberation Youth Conference, a March 1969 convention hosted by Rodolfo Gonzales's Crusade for Justice. Thanks to Shirarose Wilensky for believing in this project and whose editing helped me write a much better book.

Finally, thanks to my girlfriend, Hilary Cellini Cook, who has encouraged me for more than twenty years to keep dreaming up my stories and typing away through the night, the time when she knows I am happiest.

KARLEEN PENDLETON JIMÉNEZ is the author of Lambda Literary Award finalists *Are You a Boy or a Girl?* and *How to Get a Girl Pregnant; Tomboys and Other Gender Heroes;* and numerous short stories and essays. She wrote the award-winning animated film *Tomboy* and has been recognized by the American Library Association and the Vice Versa Awards for Excellence in the Gay and Lesbian Press. She teaches education, gender, and social justice at Trent University. Raised in Los Angeles, she lives in Toronto with her partner and daughter.

GABRIELA GODOY is an accomplished storyboard artist and illustrator living in Toronto. For the past twenty-five years, Gabi has worked with some of the best studios in Canada and Australia, including Corus Entertainment, Elliott Animation, Guru Studio, and Sticky Pictures. She considers herself extremely lucky to be able to combine her love of doodling with a natural ability to convey feelings using effortless lines to create memorable stories through animated illustration.